RUST

The Novel

CORBIN BERNSEN

Rust: The Novel
COPYRIGHT 2015 by Corbin Bernsen

All scripture quotations, unless otherwise indicated, are taken from the Holy Bible, New International Version(R), NIV(R), Copyright 1973, 1978, 1984, 2011 by Biblica, Inc.™ Used by permission of Zondervan. All rights reserved worldwide. www.zondervan.com

Cover Art by *Nicola Martinez*
Select cover photos courtesy of Home Theater Films
Emmy® is a registered trademark of the National Academy of Television Arts and Sciences. Golden Globe Award® is a registered trademark of the Hollywood Foreign Press Association. Used with Permission.

Harbourlight Books, a division of Pelican Ventures, LLC
www.pelicanbookgroup.com PO Box 1738 *Aztec, NM * 87410

Harbourlight Books sail and mast logo is a trademark of Pelican Ventures, LLC

Publishing History
First Harbourlight Edition, 2015
Paperback Edition ISBN 978-1-61116-511-1
Electronic Edition ISBN 978-1-61116-510-4
Library of Congress Control Number: 2015941522
Published in the United States of America

Dedication

For Father and Mother always.

What People are Saying
About *Rust* the Movie

"a shining story of rediscovering faith"
~Francine Brokaw of Family Magazine Group

"...all the elements of a great mystery with a helping of faith."
~ Dana Chaffin, Godandscience.org

"...spiritually uplifting and clearly shows that God will not forsake you and that His promises will be fulfilled. Dove is pleased to award *Rust* our Dove Seal for ages 12 and over."
~Dove Reviews, dove.org

"...mature and engrossing...Anyone who likes a mystery should be up for this."
~Greg Wright, Christiancinema.com

1

James Moore forced himself to blink. "I've tried. But this has to be a two-way street, and if you can't answer my simplest questions, help me at least understand where I've fallen short in your eyes…"

Silence.

Emotion balled in his throat, momentarily choked his breath. He lowered his head. The hands resting in his lap—not resting, wrung together—belonged to an old man. So many years gone, and now it had come to this? A shattered relationship that should have lasted a lifetime. He lifted his head and stared into those glassy eyes. "How can we fix this? How can we fix us…?"

Silence.

Dust motes danced in the sunbeam streaming through the window, the shaft of light mocking the darkness within him, the twirling specks oddly reminding him of a time when sitting in this humble place made him happy.

That was not today, though.

He turned his attention back to the person responsible for his tattered existence. "You're shoving me away! Don't you understand that?"

Silence.

Fear clamped its fist around his heart. Was this truly the end? What would he do?

...And like Job, a man who experienced enough pain for a hundred men, we too have our hurdles in life that seem to take great and often unfair pleasure in watching us stumble as we try to get over them...

Pastor Barrow's long-ago words filtered into James's memory. At one time, he'd believed he could clear any hurdle as long as God was with him. Now he wasn't so sure. Wasn't sure he could clear the pain. Wasn't sure God was with him. Wasn't sure about...anything.

He swallowed the lump in his throat, but it immediately returned—just one more hurdle he couldn't clear.

He lifted his gaze to those eyes again. "I love you. No less than the day I came to know you, but if you refuse to be here with me, speak to me, then I have no choice but to walk away." He despised the whine in his voice. Begging never looked good, and felt even worse. He'd given up everything for this relationship. Everything. It ending this way wasn't fair.

...But we pick ourselves up, dust off our hands and plant new seeds creating new hope. And we do so not really knowing His plan or what He has in store, but having the patience and faith to believe the reward is well worth the wait.

James shook off the memory. Regret, uncertainty, guilt converged in his gut, thick as dense fog, to cloud his resolve. Should he wait? If he gave up now, he'd lose himself; somewhere deep down, he knew that. But another part of him knew he was already lost. He had to let go. If he didn't, he'd never find himself again.

Maybe God wanted him to go.

Maybe leaving was part of God's plan...

Maybe it wasn't.

Unshed tears clouded his vision as he focused on the statue of a pleading Jesus, arms outstretched as if beckoning James into an embrace. Strange how begging seemed so pathetic when James did it, but so merciful when it came from Jesus. He'd thought he understood what that statue symbolized—the Lord's desire to embrace all, to forgive all, to befriend all—but lately James felt as though Jesus were giving him the cold shoulder. The arms on the statue might be open, but the real, live Jesus had barred His arms tight across His chest to shut James out completely, and the rejection was killing him.

There was only one solution.

He slid from the pew, stood. "I'm sorry. I can't continue like this."

He waited. Waited for the inspiration to stay. Waited for the strength to leave. Waited for any directive.

Silence.

He closed his eyes, trapped salty liquid behind eyelids heavy with grief. "I'm sorry," he whispered. "Forgive me." Turning his back on the statue, he escaped into the winter landscape of the heritage site.

The old ball field's chain-link batting cage rose into the sky, and James stood for a moment, lost in the past, seeing the children of days gone by playing games, running and shouting. Proud fathers stood behind the fence, cheering the kids. He stared, his mind swamping the plea he'd just uttered to the God he'd lost.

A kaleidoscope rushed through his memory, his mother, sitting beside him in church, listening to the preacher. He and the neighbor boy, riding a too-big bike. Watching football on their old black and white TV.

Christmases, playing hockey, all of his childhood in this small town crashed through his brain. He suddenly found himself transported to the middle of the hockey rink, lost in the past as if he'd traveled down a road and not remembered the last few miles. He replayed the days when he'd been happy just to be with his dad, when his mother had bought them cowboy hats and they'd all climbed on the tractor, Mom holding his baby sister as Dad had furrowed the rows.

And then there was the day his mother died...the minister's quiet words, his father's withdrawal, his sister's tears. His own soundless cry to heaven, wanting to know why. James couldn't go there just yet. He jerked back to the present.

Breathing in crisp winter air, he focused on the other relocated relics of his childhood, and barely gave a thought to the neatly folded black shirt he'd left on the hardwood pew—or the thin white clergy tab that had defined so much of him.

~*~

James strong-armed the steering wheel of his old pickup as wind buffeted the rusted blue steel. Windshield wipers worked double-time to keep snow flurries off the glass. Through the rearview mirror, he glanced back at the church heritage site. Ice and snow seemed to have frozen everything in history. Like the preserved buildings, his childhood triumphs on the Little League diamond, football field, hockey rink, stood motionless in his mind, just cold sculptures of joys he would never feel again.

The sun cut through the clouds offering a sliver of golden light; a possibility that this confusion, depression—whatever it was James was feeling—was only a temporary state. The timing of the show of light wasn't lost on him, and a slight twinge at the corners of his mouth almost made his lips turn upward. God certainly did move in mysterious ways—or at least, James'd think so if he wasn't convinced God was on vacation.

He glanced in the rearview mirror. Sunlight glinted off bleachers that lined the football field, bringing with it more memories. He'd loved playing sports. Didn't matter which. Baseball. Football. Hockey. He was good at them all and had the constant support of the town and his family. Superman in a world with no kryptonite.

The mental image of his father whooping and hollering, proud as any man or father could be pierced James with a double-edged blade. They'd been close then, before James had done whatever he'd done to rile his dad and create the divide between them that had dominated the last forty years. James cherished those memories of his father's love; but now those same remembrances ate him up inside. "Strained" was a sugar-coated description of a relationship as shattered as the one James now shared with his Heavenly Father.

More irony for him to tuck away and ponder later. Now wasn't the time for deep thoughts. He just wanted to get home. Who knew, maybe things would be different with Dad. Maybe he'd gotten over himself and would greet James with open arms and a fatted calf.

A grey pallor suddenly dulled the landscape as storm clouds usurped the sunlight once again.

OK, then. Message received.

The truck lurched, sending James's heart into momentary arrhythmia. He downshifted and slowed a few klicks per hour. The tires found purchase on the icy asphalt, and his heart found its steady beat. James cleared his mind and focused on the rhythmic tick of the wipers as the road disappeared beneath his tires. Keeping his mind clear of distracting memories was probably a good idea. Especially when he had so much of the present to manage.

As the cemetery came into view, James slowed the truck even more and then eased between the open gates. Sadness stalked him as he killed the engine and stepped onto undisturbed snowfall. The passage of forty-some-odd years didn't make coming here any easier. His mother's death had also marked the beginning of the end of his relationship with his father.

Wind buffeted his neck as he made his way to the grave. He shrugged a little deeper into the warmth of his favorite jacket—the only thing besides memories and faded photos that he had of his mother. How many times had she nagged him to do up the zipper? How many times had he sighed and rolled his eyes?

For her sake, he tugged on the slider, brought it a little closer to his chin. The action warmed him. Whether it was the thick fleece shutting out more of the wind or the memory of his mother, he didn't know. Maybe it was a combination of both.

He closed his eyes and listened to silence. Peace washed over him. Snow dusted his face, weighted his eyelashes for the brief moment it took to melt onto his cheeks, but the arctic chill did not disturb him. He opened his eyes to the snow-covered headstone that told anyone who cared to know that his mom had been a loving wife and mother. All true. Etched in granite for a lifetime. He smiled. He was glad to be home. The familiar made him feel safe even in the midst of all the turmoil that awaited.

He could do this, rejoin his family. He'd start fresh, renew his family ties. He'd find old friends and cement new relationships with them, catch up on the past and go forward into the future. A tiny seed of hope for a new beginning took root in his heart.

He glanced at a plot of newly dug graves. Matching headstones and surnames told James who they were. With her voice husky and somber, his sister had told him about the fire— no, "The Fire." Important. Capitalized. Emphasized. The only fire to define the entire town in all Kipling's history.

Such tragedy. He hadn't known the Pearces, but their deaths affected him just the same. He still had a hard time believing Travis had set a fire that burned up an entire family. Travis was such a gentle and innocent, beautiful soul. A person who built up others. He didn't have a destructive urge. At least, that's the way James remembered Travis.

Could his childhood best friend have changed so drastically—from beauty to beast— in James's absence?

He hoped not. But then, James had changed. Wasn't that why he was home in the first place? Because he'd had a change of heart. Had Travis lost his heart and his mind? Had he gone crazy? James stopped his thoughts. Standing in a cemetery communing with the soul of his mother wasn't the time for deep philosophical examination of Travis...or himself. Right now, he couldn't deal with what happened to Travis or his own reasons for being back home. He had other concerns to take care of, other people to see.

He said a final word to his mother and then made his way back to the truck.

Time to face his father.

2

The clink of stainless steel flatware against dishwasher-safe dinner plates clashed against the rhythmic ticking of the hall clock and disturbed the awful silence.

Had James really thought he was glad to be home? What happened to his family? This tense quiet wasn't what he was used to. These people sitting with him at the table were like strangers, like characters in some made-for-TV movie, dining in state, as if the smallest sound from any of them would break an unspoken rule with dire consequences.

He glanced at his sister as she forked a broccoli spear. She didn't look up from her plate. He wanted to start a conversation but couldn't think of a safe subject. Pick the wrong topic, and the silence wouldn't be the only disturbed thing in the room.

The weather? Hockey? School? He couldn't see any of those being good conversation starters. He didn't have a job yet, so he couldn't discuss that, either. He couldn't expound on the farm, winter was a time of rest, with little going except repairs. Repairs he hadn't helped his father with yet. Censure would follow if he brought that up.

Across from Mary, Ian sat sullen, picking at his food as if he might find bugs in it. Had James been like that at fourteen? Probably. Everything good about that year had been erased by the death of his mother. He imagined he'd been sullen. He knew he'd been confused...and empty. The vacuum borne by her departure wasn't filled, even to this day. Maybe that's why he'd failed in his vocation. How many times had he preached that God could erase all loneliness, heal all pain, calm all anger—if we let Him.

James hadn't let Him.

He had to be honest with himself. He *believed* God could do all those things, *intended* to let Him do them. Faith in that very promise was what led James to the ministry in the first place. But a part of him was afraid that if he healed completely, he'd forget her, and she'd truly be gone forever.

The revelation startled him. He *was* afraid, not *had been* afraid. Was his faith so paper-thin that he'd just been going through the motions all these years? *God, I hope not...I-I'm so sorry.* No wonder Jesus had stopped speaking to him.

He'd never let God in—not completely. Instead, he'd clung to his mother's memory as if it were the life preserver, and the pain and anger he harbored at her abandonment had fueled his direction—away from one unyielding father and towards a loving Heavenly One, or so James had thought. In reality, he'd drifted from both.

Had James's father sunken into that abyss, too? Did he believe God had taken his wife? It was a common belief amongst those who grieved that a loving God wouldn't tear lives asunder, and therefore, God must not be loving. James thought back on the times when his mother was alive, thought about the father he'd known then. Glen Moore had always been a reserved sort, but he'd smiled often when his vivacious wife goaded him into having fun. And he'd been a proud father, present at all the events James and Mary had participated in, often leaving his work early to be there. James remembered his father sometimes driving that tractor through a field at night in order to finish what he'd interrupted.

He started to look across the table at his dad but decided to avoid eye contact. The old man might sense James's inner turmoil, and that wouldn't make for appetizing dinner conversation. He was certain his father's silence was a prelude to anger. The old man had withdrawn rarely while his mother was alive, but when he had, only Mom had been able to cajole him into a better mood. James had no idea how she did it. His father would light up, his smile would tilt, and he'd be laughing in no time when his wife teased him. James didn't see himself accomplishing that any time soon.

Instead, he rested his gaze on Abigail. His seven-year-old niece was the only one at the table who seemed to be enjoying her food...but even she was quiet. Most little girls her age would be talking about princesses. He knew this because about half of his congregation's little darlings did just that. For heaven's sake, where was Abigail's tiara? Didn't most little girls wear them to the table?

Was it this stiff and cold even when James wasn't home?

He didn't think so.

Sucking in a bracing breath, he lifted his gaze to the man sitting across the table. Deep, sad lines scored his father's face. Rivulets of disappointment and days spent farming in the unforgiving sun. Emotion balled in James's gut as he studied his father's leathery skin. He ached to see the pride and love shining in Glen Moore's eyes as it had so many years past. Moments ago, James had wanted to avoid eye contact, now he willed his father to look up, erase the distance.

But more than four feet of table separated them.

James's despair lifted to heaven, even though he bade his heart to ignore God. Why, why had he gone away to become the leader of a congregation when his family needed him here? Why had he given up the town's dream that he would be its shining star—a calling card to the world acknowledging their little spec of paradise in the universe? In the end, he'd answered God's call without thought of the havoc it would wreak at home. His family, his town wallowing in hopelessness, their lives torn asunder by failure. He'd been led away…maybe by his own arrogance. Maybe he hadn't been led away by God, but by his own enthusiasm to lead a flock. Was that possible? James didn't know anymore. He'd lost his rudder, his calm in the storm, his God. His heart.

His father's eyes remained hooded, focused on nothing as far as James could tell. Not even the home-cooked meal Mary had prepared for them all. Meat, potatoes and broccoli remained untouched, unnoticed, unappreciated. How did Mary cope with this silent censure of her efforts? From his brief conversation with her earlier, James canvassed his memories to plumb the depths of his sister's emotions. She was putting on a brave front, trying to remain hopeful and smiling in the face of the divorce and her children's needs. Even then, when she was at a low point, he'd not come home. The bitterness of failing his own family galled him. James shied away from his thoughts. He looked at his father again.

Cigarette smoke curled into a haze as his father took a deep drag. The glowing red cherry sparked and then faded, the wrinkles around his father's mouth forming a well-deep sunburst. Time had not been kind to that face. Life had not been kind—to either of them.

Fleetingly, James wondered if he would look like his father in another twenty years.

There could be worse fates.

He started to speak, but his voice got lost in the scraping of chair legs across the worn linoleum floor. He clamped his lips closed as his father stubbed out the cigarette and then stood. His father's back wasn't any more inviting than his stony expression had been. No thank you for the meal, no acknowledgement of his family at all. It was as if they didn't exist. A deep anger settled in James's gut. His father was so self-absorbed he couldn't even give Mary a kind word for her efforts? And none of the others said a word. What had his family become? On previous visits, James hadn't sensed this withdrawal, this folding in of each one of them. What had changed? His mind tossed out various ideas before clarity reared its head…all those other times he'd *visited*. This time, he was staying.

James watched the man walk out the front door; then he glanced at his niece and nephew. They both seemed oblivious to their grandfather's brooding. A blessing, he supposed.

The tension in the room must have emanated only between James and his father. James willed his body to relax, dropping his shoulders, subtly stretching his legs under the table. He didn't want to think about why his staying would result in the silent treatment from his father. Turning his head, he rested his gaze on Mary, asked the silent question.

Her eyebrows raised in the slightest of movements. The facial shrug spoke volumes and said nothing all at the same time.

He gave her a wry smile—it was all he could rally. Sliding his own chair back, he got to his feet and followed his father out the door. If he was going to be home for a while—and he was—he had to get this tension cleared up before it destroyed everyone around them.

His breath curled heavily on the chill air as James exhaled. The crunch of snow under his boots was a welcome melody after the thick silence at the table. He shoved his hands into the warm pockets of his red-and-black checked jacket and trudged across the snow-packed earth to the back barn.

His father, handing some hay to the horses, didn't acknowledge James's arrival. His father had always been focused and meticulous when it came to tending his farm, but James wasn't convinced the man's mind was really on the horses. He wondered what thoughts passed through his father's head…did he relive the fleeting moments with his wife? Think on what his children had become? Worry about the future of his grandchildren? Take pride in his farm, his well-cared-for animals, or his machinery? In the lonely recesses of his mind, did Glen Moore wander lost, all life bled from him the day his wife died?

So wrapped up in his own grief, James had never really considered his father's emotions after Mom died. For the sake of family harmony, he needed to now. He shook off the lost feeling that engulfed him whenever his mother crossed his mind. His mother, so full of life, would probably be appalled at the silent, somber atmosphere that cast a pall over her family even to this day. She could coax anyone into feeling better. He didn't have her sparkling personality, but James decided he'd have to do something about bringing life and hope back into her...*his* family.

Someone needed to make the first move towards reconciliation, and it obviously wasn't going to come from the staunch and stubborn Glen Moore.

"Give you a hand with that?" James asked, keeping his tone level.

"I'm fine." His father separated out some hay.

James waited a beat. Surely, the man would look up and acknowledge his only son.

He didn't.

James heaved in a deep breath. The icy air might have chilled him if he weren't already so emotionally frozen. "We just going to keep pretending like I'm not here, or are we going to talk about this?"

"I know you're here. There's nothing to talk about."

"Oh, I don't know about that. How about how much I've disappointed you over the years?"

A gust of wind whistled by, taking a dusting of snow with it. His father gently patted the horse's muzzle and then pulled a pack of cigarettes from his pocket as he turned to face James. "I imagine whatever disappointment I'm feeling is nothing compared to what you're going through and feeling about yourself right now." He flipped open his lighter. The slight yellow flame flickered in the arctic breeze as the cigarette started to burn. His father exhaled smoke into the atmosphere. "So, I tell you what; you take care of you, and I'll take care of me." His left hand and the lighter disappeared into the pocket of his coveralls as he walked off.

James stood, stunned. He stared at the white ground, listened to his father's footfalls growing fainter, creating more distance between them. Then, he was alone. Silence again. Not even the horses made a sound, not even the breeze, which had now stilled. Alone. Abandoned. Again.

I will lead the blind on a way they do not know; by paths they do not know I will guide them. I will turn darkness into light before them, and make crooked ways straight. These are my promises: I made them, I will not forsake them.

The words from Isaiah cut a path through James's piteous disbelief. He was on a journey, on a path unrecognized, and blind to God's reasons for allowing him to experience—to endure—this brokenness with the one person who should be the most supportive. But with the shred of faith still sparking his soul, James understood that if he endured, if he allowed God the time, the Lord could bring about restoration and healing. James had only to be patient and pliable.

Two things that had never come easy to him.

A smile tugged his lips as the realization hit him that he was like his father in that way. Some common ground on which to build, even if his father wasn't quite ready to trudge that mutual path just yet.

A horse nickered as the wind picked up. James stood against the buffeting air and embraced the winter along with the challenges that lay ahead.

Determination. Another trait that had been passed from father to son.

~*~

James guided the truck across the unpaved, narrow back road. Crowded between Mary and him in the front seat of the pickup, Ian retained his sullenness while Abigail chattered on about a story the teacher had told her at school. His niece's enthusiasm was infectious, and James smiled as he glanced at the passing landscape. Acres of flat farmland hidden under a blanket of untouched snow.

In the distance, the charred remains of a farmhouse came into view. As they approached, James slowed the truck to take a look. Part of a wall and the chimney stood firm, as though the bricks had forgotten to fall along with the rest of the building. Splintered, blackened wood jutted up at odd angles among the debris as if reaching for the sky in a silent plea for…what? Supplication? Mercy? A savior?

A small fountain of anger crossed James's mind. He'd broken off that relationship with God. He needed to train his brain to not automatically turn to a Lord Who had stopped giving him answers. It wasn't that he didn't believe…he'd just stopped believing God would provide the answers. He had to deal with his problems himself, to face whatever was in front of him and take it on by himself. With an effort, James forced his thoughts towards yet another problem he should address.

Had Travis caused this devastation? James shook his head in answer to his own silent question. It was unfathomable. The Travis he remembered had been easy-going, constantly laughing, always in good spirits. He'd been so happy all the time that people gravitated to him, basking in his joy and innocence, regardless of the fact that his naïveté was a byproduct of mental challenges that Travis, in just being Travis, somehow made irrelevant.

"It's been real hard on everyone," Mary said quietly, as if speaking any louder would breach some code of reverence. "Especially the kids." The break in her voice emphasized her point.

A million questions traipsed through James's mind—Did anyone notice Travis changing? Did anyone ask him if he needed help? Did Travis know he'd turned into a monster? And above all those questions was a simple why? Why did this happen to good people? Why was the rug ripped out from under those who were just beginning to hope again?—but he wouldn't ask any of those questions here, in front of the kids.

"They're in heaven now," Abigail said.

James turned from the window and glanced at his family.

Abigail peered back at him, seemingly unaffected by the obvious tragedy. That was a good thing. Seven-year-olds weren't supposed to be traumatized by the horrors that life could inflict. Her faith in the adults, in the world, was intact. For the first time, James wondered if Abigail and Ian believed in God. Had Mary taken them to church? He chastised himself...had he ever taken them to church during his fleeting visits? He was as guilty of not taking care of his family's spiritual needs as anyone. As a son, a brother, an uncle—a pastor—he should have been here, present for his family, so when the pieces fell apart, he could have comforted them, counseled them. Instead, he was hundreds of miles away. What was it 1 Timothy 5:8 said? *But if any provide not for his own, and especially for those of his own house, he hath denied the faith, and is worse than an infidel.* More failure. It burned in James's heart. He couldn't look inside there anymore.

Mary's focus was past him and on the burned farmhouse that marred the pristine landscape. Her expression reflected ever difficult emotion a mother could feel: pain, despair, fear. Her haunted face dug deep into James's soul, resting there against the emotions he'd just buried.

Ian's stony expression gave nothing of the boy's feelings.

James turned back to the window. "What—"

"Mom, can we just go," Ian blurted.

His nephew's vehemence gave James pause for a moment. The boy had spent the evening in emotionless silence. Why would this scene ignite such a fiery response? Had he been friends with one of the children? Survivor's guilt? As a counselor to his flock, James was used to people coming to him for advice, pouring out their troubles. Oftentimes, their grief had built in their minds until it swamped all other feelings and the only solution was to confess before God, or His representative. A calling to which James could no longer lay claim. But maybe he could help his nephew as a secular counselor, as an uncle. Maybe this was the avenue God created to allow James back into His grace. Maybe here is where James would find his own heart, his own soul, and return to his God. *Is this it, God? The thing You want me to do so Your healing can make us all whole?*

Making a mental note to probe a little deeper, James put the truck in gear and drove the rest of the way to Mary's house. He didn't want to think on that little flicker of hope in his heart in case he did something stupid to squash the tiny spark that rose from the ashes of desolation.

He pulled the truck to a stop outside his sister's house. Toys littered the front yard, and the mobile home had visibly weathered since James was home last. He wondered if Mary was really doing as well after her divorce as she claimed. The property might not be high-maintenance compared to some, but she was a middle-aged single mother of two who now worked a full-time job. How did she manage to keep up? Especially since her husband had traded her in for the proverbial younger model. In a town as small as Kipling, that had to smart even more than if Mary'd been able to remain anonymous in a sea of city dwellers.

Guilt swamped him again. While he was gone, his family had deteriorated. While he'd been off tending to other people's needs, his own family had slipped into this cold landscape of the heart. He'd known it would take effort to seamlessly slip back into his family, but he'd not expected them to be so...reserved.

No, that wasn't the right word. James faced it straight on. Unhappy. His entire family was smothered with unhappiness, as if life no longer held hope.

Mary smiled, but behind that was pain. Ian retreated from everyone before he could be pushed away. James recognized that from his years of counseling teens. His father was...James had never understood his father's visage. Only Abigail acted happy, and James suspected that was because the little girl didn't notice or feel the seething tide of emotions that swirled above her understanding.

Mary muscled open the rusty blue door and reminded James of happier times. She'd never been able to open that door easily. A hundred years ago, it was because she was slight, and the door heavy. Now that Mary was capable, the ancient, rusted hinges didn't have the wherewithal to cooperate. James smiled easily as he watched her slide out of the truck.

Abigail and Ian followed. Ian jogged across the lawn and disappeared into the house. His sister hung back and looked up at their mother with expectant eyes.

"Run inside, sweetie. Get to your homework. I'll be right there."

Without answering her mother, Abigail hopped back inside the truck and threw her arms around James for a quick hug; then she slid back out and headed for the house.

Mary closed the truck door and rested a hand on the open window.

"She's got good spirit," James said.

"Oh, I've got a few other names for it." Mary grinned at him. Her pride in Abigail shone on her face. There was the Mary he knew and loved. The one who had nothing more than delight on her face.

James studied his sister. He'd missed her. Missed the kids. Maybe now he was back, he could help out a little. Do some maintenance around the house, help babysit or chauffeur. If God had put him here to mend relationships, the best way to start was by mending what was broken on the outside. He could borrow tools from his father...or maybe he'd just visit a hardware store to pick up a few essentials.

"For what it's worth, I'm glad you're back. Everyone's missed you," she said.

He nodded. "It'll be great to get to know Ian and Abigail."

"She wants to be called Abby now."

"Abby." James had been about thirteen when he'd decided he didn't want to be called Jimmy. Too old for such a baby name, he'd said. Now, he didn't care a whit. Jimmy, Jim, James...whatever. He wondered how long it would be before Abigail's preference evaporated.

He looked deep into his sister's eyes. He wasn't much for showing emotion, but maybe if he stared deep enough she'd figure out how much he cared. "I look forward to spending some time with both of them."

Mary smiled. "I know they'd like that." She glanced past him and then took a heavy breath. "So," she said, focusing on him again, "you think you'll be here for a while this time?"

Her question stabbed him. The evidence that his family couldn't even trust his word when he said he'd come home to stay, showed how deeply his leaving had affected them all. He deserved this. The emptiness, the distance, the isolation. And he'd have to do more to make them understand he was a man of Go...no, he didn't belong to God anymore. But he could still be a man of his word. He was obviously still good at the poker face, because Mary didn't seem to sense his troubled thoughts. Good. "That's the plan." He finally smiled, playing it nonchalant.

He searched her face for reassurance as the image of their father materialized in his mind. Glen Moore wasn't glad James was home. But James would change that—he hoped. "I don't recall him being like that...Dad...so angry."

"Oh, Jimmy, it's been tough on him. For a long time. And then with the fire."

"I can imagine." He glanced away so she wouldn't catch the platitude. He could imagine only to a degree. There was an honest part of him that couldn't imagine at all. No matter what a man was going through, he shouldn't shut out his only son.

The fire was what was on everyone's

mind. Yet, as far as James could tell, most of the folks he'd seen and talked to didn't seem to really know the Pearces. What made them all feel so guilty? Had they realized how fleeting life could be? Had some, in light of the tragedy, tried to reconcile with family, only to be rebuffed? Had they tried to change their own lives, only to discover, as he had with God and with his father, that it was too late? Or was it that their idyllic little town had been besmirched by the fact that some of their own had died needlessly at the hands of someone they'd all thought to be harmless?

Questions swirled in his brain until he shut them off. There was so much need here, so much need in himself, so much need in his father, his sister, his niece and nephew, this entire town was one huge ball of need. They needed hope and a future.

James's soul cried for all the need in front of him. He was so broken he couldn't even help them. It would take One far more powerful than he was—

"It's just horrible. It's been real horrible. Just so sad," Mary said, drawing James's attention.

For a long, silent moment, he tried to think of an appropriate response. He wanted to ask specifics about how horrible it had been—

the economy, the fire, his dad's loneliness and disappointment in his only son—but words wouldn't form, and the tension billowed between them. He didn't want bad blood between his sister and him, but he'd broken her trust in him. He'd have to fix this issue. Bitterness rose towards the God who'd led him to shepherd other flocks and left his own family bereft.

Mary let out a puff of breath. "You've got to put it all in perspective, look at the bigger picture. When you left, you confused a lot of people. Not just Dad. What you did with yourself, ministering His word, of course we're all proud of that. I mean, it's not like you ran off and joined the circus."

"Not so sure about that, but go on."

"But for some people, lots of people, you were the...I don't know, *hope*, for us. The difference. They expected something bigger from you, I guess. Something to make us stick out in the world and say, 'hey, here we are.'"

"I can't believe everyone put so much stock in me." And, he didn't want to believe it. To believe that meant he had let down more than his father, more than God Who expected James to keep his vow—more than his sister standing here now so sweet and understanding, so strong and capable when he, the elder, was a weakened wreck.

"Well, they did. And don't pretend you don't know that. And it's not something a short visit every couple of years makes any better. Could even make it worse, I suppose." She searched his face as if waiting for an answer he had no ability to provide.

Disappointment dulled her eyes. "So now, here you are again, only this time you come back when everyone could really use a lift... a little reassurance that this terrible thing that's happened to us has some bigger purpose. And you, of all people, given what you left here to do, might be the one to give us that faith. I suppose people are just confused and disappointed all over again."

Frustration curled into his throat. He wasn't everyone's savior, had never signed on for such a mission. It wasn't fair to pressure that kind of expectation on him. "And what makes you think I'm not just as confused and disappointed as everyone else?"

She studied him quietly for a moment, and the compassion he saw settle into her expression dissipated some of his irritation.

"I don't know," she said softly. "Things have been just so...bad, not just for us, Jim, but everyone. Rust has been real bad last couple of crops. Then this fire. The Pearces, it's funny, well not funny, but they came here five years ago from England—England no less—took over the Parker farm, and showed us a spirit like, I don't know, they just so loved being here and farming and working the land. The Pearce boy, he was maybe twelve and actually wanted to grow up to be a farmer like his dad. And that's rare these days! His daughter was a few years older, really pretty. She fit right in with the other kids in town. Real pretty gal. Such a shame. Just makes no sense."

Mary got quiet for a moment, and time stretched across the cab of the truck as James tried to envision this family who had come all the way from...*England?*...and been accepted only to be struck down.

He marveled that they'd come to America, even when rust threatened the crops. No wonder people loved them. He remembered his father and others keeping diligent watch for the disease in their fields. The rust colored fungus was called the "polio" of the wheat crops, spreading like wildfire if not controlled quickly. Mr. Pearce must have really loved the land to come into a community knowing they'd had a fatal crop disease affecting their ability to sell their wheat. That took dedication. Dedication fostered hope. James had lost dedication to the One who'd influenced his life the most, he couldn't bring hope to his own family, much less the whole town. As despair anchored in his heart, a glimmer of realization dared to spark.

Maybe he *had* returned to Kipling to rekindle hope for this town, and for himself—to rekindle hope in God. Was that what God was trying to say to this lost flock?

But how could God use him, a broken vessel the Lord no longer acknowledged, to bring peace to an entire town? It just didn't seem possible. Guilt, anger, fear, doubt...it all cluttered James's heart, extinguishing the glimmer. He was no one. He couldn't be great; he'd not even lived up to the potential people saw in him as a teenager. He was middle-aged now, what could they possibly expect from a has-been preacher who couldn't even hang on to his faith?

"He was real hard working, Mr. Pearce, and a good Christian." Mary's voice pulled James out of his thoughts. "He was a little tough on his kids, especially the daughter—real strict with her—but he genuinely seemed to embrace the opportunity of being here. Started to lift everyone's spirits...Then..." His sister's voice trailed off even as it captured his attention.

The silence returned.

James couldn't fathom the depth of influence this Pearce family had had on the whole of Kipling, but regardless of his inadequate understanding, he could see clearly the pain carved in the lines on his sister's face. He wanted to reach out to her, physically, emotionally, spiritually, but his own brokenness arrested any action or words. His heart was void. Until he could find healing and guidance for himself, how could he hope to help his family, this town? Guilt at his own faithlessness settled deeper.

I will praise You, for I am fearfully and wonderfully made; Marvelous are Your works, and that my soul knows very well.

The Psalm reverberated so loud, James glanced towards his sister, wondering if she heard it.

"Hey, I better let you go," he said, finally.

A flicker of disappointment flashed across her face and then recoiled to knock him in the gut. He blinked it away and heaved in a breath, but didn't speak. What was there to say that wouldn't aggravate the wounds, make them split open and deepen?

She crunched her mouth into a forced sweet smile and gave him a slight nod fueled by the resignation reflected in her eyes. With a tap to the window frame, she turned and walked away. Her hunched shoulders showed a palpable anguish.

His heart flooded with so many emotions, he couldn't do anything more than blink back tears. I'm not the man you think I am, Mary. I'm not that hero. I never was. How can anyone put such stock in me? I left here, I left you all to battle the rust, to battle the losses, to battle the disappointments alone...I'm no hero...I'm just a man...one who came here to find solace...only to find you all need what I can't even give.

He watched her go inside before he popped the truck into gear and headed down the road.

3

Diffused early morning light sparkled in the frosty condensation on the truck's hood. James turned down the dirt drive and bumped along the road to the charred remains of the Pearce farmhouse. The rumbling engine seemed to disturb the reverence that James instinctively afforded the scene—so much so that he was grateful to cut the noise and slide out of the pickup.

A few birds chirped from some hidden place as if in tribute to the lives once living in this scorched, desolate place. The breeze whispered past James's ear as he studied the blackened remains.

It's been real horrible. His sister's words from yesterday seeped into his mind. Horrible. When had Travis ever done anything *horrible?* The figure of Travis, his smile, the water boy, loping out to meet James and the team on the high school football field after a win dissolved his sister's words and their implication. The innocent teen with the disheveled hair and quirky clothes could not have done this. His heart was too soft, too selfless. No matter how often James tried to picture it, the images just wouldn't form. Travis might be odd, but he wasn't dangerous, and until James heard the confession from Travis's own lips, he wouldn't believe it—maybe not even then.

So, what had truly happened here?

After one last look at the macabre scene, James climbed back into his truck and headed for the KMI. An appetizing breakfast at the Kipling Motor Inn's diner would set him for the day ahead. A day he intended to complete by proving his friend's innocence and finding out what really happened at the Pearce farm.

~*~

Hushed conversation permeated the bustle of the coffee shop as James walked through the glass doors. The frigid air that wafted in with him immediately warmed, and he felt a moment of fleeting hominess. He unzipped his jacket and shrugged out of it.

"Just the one of you?"

The young, dark-haired hostess didn't look familiar, and it hit him just how long he'd been away this time. He smiled. "Yes. Thank you."

He followed her across the worn and dingy tile flooring and then pulled out a red vinyl chair at the table she indicated. He took in the laminate wood wall paneling and the cracked Venetian blinds. This place hadn't changed since he was here last, hadn't changed much since high school as far as he could tell.

"Coffee?"

"Please," he answered. "Thank you.

She plopped the menu on the table and left.

James scanned the restaurant, his gaze resting on an older man and woman who were staring at him from across the way. He nodded, and they returned the gesture. Cordial enough, but James noticed the covert glances in his direction as the couple resumed their conversation. He didn't allow the scrutiny to bother him. This was a small town, he'd been gone a long time—and not because he was off playing pro ball and bringing glory to the town that had supported him through his high school career. A little gossip was bound to blossom, especially now, considering it was common knowledge that he and Travis were best friends. Just one more item to fuel the scandal pyre.

His gaze traveled to some of the other tables. Tentative nods, fleeting smiles, and furtive looks greeted him. Giving a mental shrug, he willed himself not to feel uncomfortable and then lifted the menu to study the selection.

Suddenly, a strong arm captured James in a headlock. "Guess who."

He couldn't think. The affected deep voice didn't sound familiar, although, it had to be someone James knew; he could still breathe, so whoever it was, wasn't trying to strangle him in the middle of the KMI for all to witness. "I don't know," James answered.

The chokehold pressure increased. "Come on, guess! Feel that muscle closing down on your throat. Who could that be?"

"I don't…seriously, I can't breathe…"

The grip cinched a little tighter. "And you're gonna blackout in about two seconds unless you make a guess."

The guy was right. The pressure building in his head made his brain feel like a squeezed orange. Stars were beginning to form in his eyes. Maybe if he could focus, he'd be able to make a—

"Let him go, Duane, before he passes out."

"Duane?" James choked out as he looked to Loretta. His old friend wielded a carafe of coffee and a satirically stern expression.

The pressure on his head released and a rush of blood made him momentarily dizzy. Duane Jack slid around the table and sat opposite James, a huge grin spread across his face.

The sheriff had aged a bit since James was home last, but even so, stilled looked younger than his true age—which Duane refused to divulge. His girlish secrecy had been a constant source of teasing back in the day, especially considering how masculine Duane really was, wrestling trophies, and all.

"How's it going, preach?"

"Coffee, Duane?" Loretta slipped in.

"Black would be beautiful."

"Thanks, Loretta," James said.

She grinned at him and offered a salute with the glass coffee carafe and then filled the white porcelain mugs. "You're looking handsome as ever, Jimmy." She winked and then walked off.

James moved his attention to the man across the table. The tan uniform and its accoutrements made Duane look formidable.

"Wow! Everyone was starting to think you'd forgotten about us. We usually get you at least two, three times a decade. Been a while, stranger."

James smiled, the tension falling from his

shoulders for the first time in days. "You darn near killed me." He rubbed his neck for effect.

Humor lit Duane's gaze and reminded James of the good times they'd shared as teens.

"And I woulda if Loretta hadn't stepped in and saved your sorry butt." Duane glanced at James, the humor dulling. "Man oh man. It's good to see you, Jimmy. Seriously. I hear you might be sticking around for a while."

"That's the plan." James caught movement in his peripheral; his attention pulled to a table across the way. The woman quickly lowered her head. A man at a different table did the same. As his gaze traveled back to his friend at the other side of the table, the scrutiny of so many pricked James in the gut.

"Good to hear it. Good to hear that." Duane sipped on his coffee, evidently oblivious to the other town-folk or James's discomfort.

James cleared his throat of the unease. "Hey, you want to get out of here?" He leaned across the table. "I want to know about Travis, but not in here…"

Duane rested both forearms across the edge of the Formica table and dipped his head low.

"C'mon, Duane," James urged, not quite understanding his friend's obvious reluctance. He still couldn't fathom that even the mention of Travis's name made people nervous.

Duane took a quick, covert glance at the room and then gave a slight, almost imperceptible nod. He sighed. "OK, buddy."

The words were so hushed that it took James a moment to register Duane's answer.

James pulled out a few bills and left enough money on the table for his and Duane's meals and then they stepped into the winter stillness outside the diner. The never-changing town had sadly changed since James's last trip home. Boarded windows and empty buildings lined the main street. Shrouded by the grey sky, deserted storefronts mirrored the vacancy of spirit that James had felt from the moment he arrived.

A lone worker, bundled in a stocking cap and winter parka, perched high on a ladder hanging Christmas decorations on a streetlamp. The festoon seemed an oddity against the somber atmosphere, and James thought of Travis more deeply. "Tell me," he said simply.

"We all knew it was coming. Only a matter of time, and then…well, you saw the place, right? Burned to the ground. They were good people, the Pearces."

Good people. Wasn't Travis "good people?" Like a needle stuck on a warped vinyl record, he silently asked again what had happened.

"Where's Travis at?"

"Over in Bishop," Duane answered as they crossed the street and headed towards the hockey rink. "The psychiatric place there. They're doing some sort of evaluation—competency stuff the court ordered."

"Then what?"

Duane let out a heavy sigh and stopped walking. "Oh, I don't know. And frankly, Jimmy, I don't care. It's out of my hands now."

James came up short and turned to face his friend.

Duane dropped his gaze to the snowpack under their feet. "The Travis you knew and what he became"—he glanced at James's face—"day and night. Especially the last couple years." He straightened and a resoluteness settled over his expression as he squared James in the eye. "What was once weird but cute just became...I don't know...weird. Weirder. We should've got him to a place he fit in a long time ago." Duane took a step forward. "We all have to take some of the blame for not dealing with it." He shook his head and walked past James. "Just a matter of time, and here we are."

James let the words seep in. Could this tragedy have been avoided if he'd been around to see the signs? Travis had taken James's leaving pretty hard, that much James knew.

"So how about you?" Duane's words cut into James's thoughts. "What happened to you?"

James gave a slight chuckled. If only he had the answer to that question. "I wish I knew," he said.

"You just woke up one day and said, 'Sorry, Lord, but I do believe this dance is over'?"

James shrugged. "Something like that."

"Wow. I imagine that's going to be a messy divorce."

James smiled at that, but the humor quickly faded as the ironic reality of Duane's words hit him with gale force. Messy was an understatement. His life was shredded into such tiny strips he didn't know if it could ever be restitched into a recognizable pattern. Who in his right mind divorced God? Was that even possible without doing irreparable damage to the soul?

Duane reached for the door to the rink and pulled it open. The scrape of skate blades against the ice mingled with the clack of hockey sticks. A whistle blew and the shouts of a coach echoed through the hall.

James and Duane climbed the bleachers and settled in to watch the scrimmage. The game started and a single boy caught James's attention. He recognized Duane's son as the kid raced down the ice gliding the puck along the smooth surface of the ice.

"Remind you of anyone," Duane asked.

James glanced at Duane, took note of the pride shining in Duane's eyes. "He's good. Much better than I ever was."

"Not so sure about that, but he *is* good."

Carter passed the puck just as he got checked. No penalty whistle blew.

"He want to go pro?" James asked.

Duane shrugged one shoulder. "Which one of them down there doesn't? But he may actually have a shot...and I'm not just saying it 'cause I'm his old man."

James chuckled at that. "Of course not."

"Seriously. There've been guys calling about him. Scouts. But who knows."

Who knew about anything anymore, James thought. Even the things he thought were guaranteed didn't seem so etched in stone anymore. "I'm going to see Travis."

"I figured you would." Duane shook his head. "He's not the guy you remember, Jimmy. He's not little Travis the water boy no more. He ain't 'Toad.' No sir. He's just been getting weirder and weirder and weirder, especially in the last couple years. Some folks could barely tolerate it any more. Ol' man Riley over at the pharmacy has been all over my tail to do something about it. You can believe I'm taking some heat here for what happened."

Carter, in possession of the puck once again, drove the black disc into the net.

"Atta boy, Carter!" Duane yelled.

"I don't get it," James said. "What do you mean? How's he so different from before. I mean, OK, he's Travis, we all know that—"

"Well, where do you want to start?" A troubling hint of irritation edged Duane's tone. "How about he got to wearing a...what do you call those little dresses ballet girls wear?"

"A tutu?"

"Right. He'd put on a pink one of them things in the middle of the night, didn't matter—freeze-your-pants-off-cold-dead-of-winter—and go prancing down Main Street. Middle of the night twirling around like a fairy princess while we're all asleep. It could be twenty below." Duane shook his head. "One screw at a time his whole head's come loose."

"His wardrobe was always a little different. We all knew that."

Duane let out a grunt of disbelief. "Are you hearing me? Yes, we tolerated the fact that he didn't bathe much and dressed like a moron. This ain't that."

James just stared, unable to reconcile the

person Duane was describing with the person James knew Travis to be.

"Look, I can't talk about this right now, just makes me sick. It's too raw. We shoulda done something for him when we had a chance, and we didn't. We thought it was endearing. Now what's done is done, and it can't be undone. There's no good part to this story, Jim. Not for Toad, not for any of us."

James traveled through is memories. Travis *was* endearing. Gentle. Sweet. Thoughtful. Childlike in mind if not in body. *We shoulda done something for him.* Duane's words ricocheted in James's mind. What should they have done for Travis? He wasn't broken, just mentally challenged—just different. How could his innocent quirks and peculiarities have morphed into something dangerous and deadly?

…Unless he'd been driven to it.

4

Skyscrapers jutted into the skyline as the city of Bishop came into view. James's heartbeat kicked it up a notch. By nature, not much made him nervous, but today he was terrified of what he might discover. Believing Travis's innocence came easy, even with the sight of the devastated farmhouse, but what would James do if Travis confessed right here? Right now. To James's face. The implications touched his heart, burrowed into his mind. He automatically reached out for the One he used to lean on, before he remembered he'd given up on God. His soul cried at the emptiness within.

He navigated through city traffic and turned down the tree-lined drive that led to Bishop Psychiatric Facility. Traffic noise and city bustle faded into the distance, and the resulting stillness allowed James to calm his nerves. Anxiety shouldn't even be a factor. Travis was innocent. The boy had always been innocent, and him growing into a man, didn't change that. James steeled his conviction. He didn't have to fear what Travis would say.

He'd never been to the BPF before, and as he rounded the property and tucked into a parking space, he hoped he'd never have to come again. The stone building stood formidable against a blue sky. Barred windows and a center tower made it look more like a formidable castle keep than a hospital. All it lacked was a moat to keep out intruders—or to keep the inmates confined—appropriate James supposed, since many of the patients were the criminally insane. Travis…in this place, with people who would never understand the innocence of his heart and mind.

James killed the car engine and pulled the keys from the ignition. For a moment he just sat, calming the nerves that rattled his mind. Once again, he told himself that he had nothing to fear. Travis was innocent.

But if that were true…Don't go there, James.

He got out of the truck and shoved the keys into his left pocket. With a deep, fortifying breath filling his lungs, he put one foot in front of the other.

Once inside, an orderly led him down a narrow hallway. Rooms on either side were secured with stereotypical grey steel doors that featured small, square panes of safety glass. A disconcerting feeling settled over him, but he told himself it was psychosomatic. In all his years as a pastor, he'd never seen the inside of a mental institution and, unbidden, horror stories both real and imagined traipsed through his head. He willed away the eerie feelings and told himself he was being ridiculous. No one was strapped to a gurney getting an unwarranted lobotomy—but he didn't try to see inside the rooms. Avoidance? Or fear?

Strange how one's mind went in odd directions. He took a mental note to ponder that later. He couldn't remember being so out of sorts at any time during his pastorate, or before—when he was regularly engaged in conversations with Jesus. Was there a correlation?

James gritted his teeth. If there was a correlation, he was irritated. It was Jesus, after all Who'd quit talking to James, not the other way around.

Almost to the end of the corridor, the orderly unlatched a door and motioned for James to enter the room. He hesitated a moment and took a fleeting glance down to the end of the hall to note that it opened into a spacious area where a few staff and several obvious patients roamed. For a microsecond he wondered if Travis was allowed to be out in the open or if they kept him caged.

He shuddered at the thought and then entered the waiting room. Without speaking a word, the orderly closed the door and disappeared. The door's closure made a sudden claustrophobia rear up, but James tamped it down. He wouldn't be left here in this building. He was just a visitor.

James took a seat at the lone metal table in the middle of the room and looked at the empty chair across from him. The impact of where he was—and why he was here—hit him like a sledgehammer to the ribs, and his resolve almost caved. *Lord, please help me get through this. Help me get to the bottom of this mess.*

Why was he praying? God had quit listening to him a long time ago. The stark fluorescent lighting did nothing to cheer the drab cinderblock walls, and James closed his eyes to them. An image of Travis lying on the autumn earth, head-to-head with James and looking into a beautiful sky emerged in James's mind.

"What do you s'pose is up there, Travis?"

"You mean besides clouds and God?"

"Yeah."

"I don't know. Maybe Mrs. God."

Their laughter reverberated in James's mind even to this day, bringing with it the warmth of the friendship he shared with Travis. Pieces of his heart shattered with those memories. This...this *thing* of which Travis was accused, no way could he have done it.

In James's mind's eye, Travis grew into a teen. Varsity football water boy and overall morale-booster. He took pride in his simple duties, pride in being part of the team.

"I just can't connect, Travis. It's like my arm's a lead weight. It won't do what I'm asking it to."

"Then quit talking to it, Jimmy, and play the game. Play the game."

Who'd shown leadership insight that day? James-the-star-QB or Travis-the-waterboy? Even in matters Travis couldn't possibly know first-hand, he'd held a wisdom that belied his mental acuity. Maybe it was his innocence and simplicity that made it so, but whatever it was, it had helped Travis become James's voice of reason on more occasions than James could count. Would they have even won that game that day if it hadn't been for Travis's basic, but somehow profound, advice?

The door opened, drawing James's attention. Guided by the orderly, Travis shuffled in with his head bowed and his scruffy hair shrouding his face. The standard-issue coveralls hung loose on his body, making him look like a child playing dress-up. He lifted his head a little and set his gaze on James. Eyes the color of rich chocolate reflected the innocence and joy James remembered, and Travis's perpetual smile gave no hint that he might be feeling the pressure most would experience at being incarcerated.

The orderly pulled out the chair opposite James and then guided Travis to sit. "I'll be outside," he said. "You behave, Travis."

Travis looked up at the man, an amused glow lighting his features. "Aye aye, Cap'n." He turned his attention to James and beamed a grin that shot joy across the table and wrapped James in a cocoon of assurance.

It was strange how Travis could have such a calming effect on people without even trying.

"Pretty messed up, huh?" Travis said around a tongue that seemed too big for his mouth.

"Yeah. Pretty messed up." James nodded slightly, suddenly feeling a little awkward. He hadn't expected to dive right in—why, he didn't know; Travis never minced words or beat around the bush, or any of those other clichés that people fell into in order to avoid the tough subjects.

"Well, you're lookin' good. I got all your

letters." He motioned with his head as if the envelopes were stashed in the corner of the room. "I save 'em. My mom has them at the house in a box."

"Good. I'm glad to hear that." James scrutinized Travis for a moment trying to spot any concealed rage or ill intent. James shook his head. Travis was still just Travis. James relaxed a little and rested his forearms across the metal table. "Are you OK?"

Travis's smile faded as he lifted one shoulder in a brief shrug. "I guess." For a moment, a load as heavy as all the troubles in Kipling seemed to weigh on that slight body. But as quickly as James noticed it, it was gone.

Travis's trademark smile beamed across the table, and his eyes lit with sudden excitement. "Suppose you want to know what happened."

James lifted his palms and shook his head. "No. It's O—"

"I don't mind." Travis shook his head as the words rushed out, his gaze focused but still glowing with innocence. "I don't remember a whole bunch, only doin' it."

The words stole James's breath. Travis was innocent. How could he remember doing it if he didn't do it at all? And yet, his words were so blunt. Unmistakable. Travis had always been that straightforward, that hadn't changed.

Confusion and fear brewed an odd concoction in James's gut. He shifted in the chair, becoming acutely aware of the hard molded plastic. He had to rein his emotions. He was a trained counselor. He knew how to handle unexpected and emotional situations, with poise. He forced a reassuring smile and prayed to his absent God that the curve of his lips looked genuine and not as plastic as the chairs that flanked the cold metal table.

Travis smiled back, apparently oblivious to James's slip of composure.

"Used a cigarette to get it goin'. Then they came, and I told them what I done; and then they took me away. But they been pretty good to me. Considering."

James blinked. Once. Twice. Was he missing something? A secret code? A hidden meaning in Travis's words that in reality meant, "I have no idea how the fire got going" or "I've been framed, Jimmy. Help me out of this mess".

"So what about you? I hear you got some news of your own. My mom said you come back 'cause you quit preaching. She said you run out of 'Jesus juice.'"

James chuckled at that. He shouldn't be so surprised that even in here, Travis knew what was going on in town. James nodded slightly.

"Something like that."

"Well then, I guess we both got our problems."

An involuntary smile curved James's lips as deep understanding flowed like a balm over his body. Travis had done it again—eased all anxiety with a simple, but profound truth that was beyond the man's own level of comprehension. James had often contemplated the possibility that Travis had a direct line to God, to make up for what he lacked otherwise.

Yes, they both had their problems. And there was only one thing to do about that.

Deal with them.

He scooted back the chair and moved to the barred window while he tried to gather his thoughts. Snow fell to the ground in a thick sheet of flakes obscuring the view beyond a few scant feet—Like in here, where the truth was obscured behind a thick blanket of doubt.

"Looks like we're getting dumped on pretty good."

James turned and stared at Travis, bemused by the man's calm exterior. What was going on in Toad's mind? Was that absolute peace a gift from God? Or was it because Travis had no idea of the implications of his plight?

"Hey, don't suppose you could oil the chain on my old bike? She's one of my favorites. Rescued her from the dump and worked real hard on her, and the damp will just...do her in."

James struggled for patience. He wanted Travis to give him some straight answers, but the guy's mind just flitted from one thing to the next. He let out a heavy sigh. It wasn't Toad's fault, yet his inability to focus was frustrating. Travis lived in the moment, he didn't have the foresight to plan anything...especially setting a fire that killed. Once again, James wondered how he could clear Travis's name without any help or understanding at all—not even from Travis, himself.

He moved back to the table and leaned across it, got in Travis's face. "You still haven't answered my question."

"I told you."

"No, you didn't!" He straightened and pulled off his jacket. "Travis, listen. I want you to tell me everything that happened exactly. Everything that happened that night after you left the game at Taft." He chunked his coat across the table and studied Travis in earnest. If he looked like he meant business, maybe Travis would open up more, explain...let something slip the police may have not heard or understood. Something that would clear him. Something James could investigate, could grab hold of, could actively pursue instead of sitting here helpless as a baby.

Travis sucked in a deep breath and then scanned the room as if searching for conspirators. For a brief moment, James thought he was about to hear the truth, but then Travis dug into the pockets of his coveralls and pulled out a pack of cigarettes.

He eyed James as he lit one and took in a deep drag.

"You allowed to have those in here?" James asked.

"No, but what're they gonna do? Put me in jail?"

Travis snickered, but James wasn't amused. Somehow, he had to get Travis to understand just how grave his situation was.

Travis sobered and looked at James directly. "OK. Normally I stay around after a game, you know how I do, win or lose I want to be there for the boys. But this time, fourth quarter ended, horn went off, and I just got on my bike and got out of there as fast as I could. Got on my bike and started riding. I was so mad. I was ridin' real fast! I was mad 'cause we lost, and we shouldn't have. Those boys got no heart, not like you used to. I was real mad, Jimmy!" His words ground out on a grunt rife with frustration.

He paused to suck in a quick, noisy drag on the cigarette, blew out slowly a steady stream of misty smoke. "Then all that road went by, and I didn't even notice, and next thing you know I seen it from the road, the Pearce place. Everybody liked him, Mr. Pearce, but he had a mean streak. He didn't like me. He pretended to but he didn't." Travis words strung together as his story became more vehement.

"What do you mean, 'he didn't like you?'" James kept his tone even, his expression stoic. Clearly Travis felt affronted by the Pearce patriarch, but James needed Travis to stay focused and unagitated.

"I don't know," Travis shot out around his thick tongue. "He just didn't. He pretended to be nice, but I know what he was thinking." Travis was insistent.

"And what was that?"

"'Boy it sure would be nice to get rid of Travis. Take him over to that recycling plant where he works and recycle him.' Never liked me from the day he moved here with his fancy accent. I could tell. His wife was nicer. So were the kids..." His voice trailed off as he bowed his head. It was trait Travis had exhibited before when he'd messed up. Was he upset that he said something mean about Mr. Pearce, or did it go deeper? Was that remorse? At killing the kids?

A pit opened up in the middle of James's stomach and dread churned acid inside. Only a guilty man could feel remorse. Remorse was the flip side of guilt...if one had a properly-formed conscience, anyway. But remorse didn't pair with innocence. Innocent people could be empathetic, sympathetic, sad, but not remorseful. *Oh, Lord, please don't let Travis be guilty of this. There has to be some other rational explanation. Not guilt. Not guilt!* James's soul screamed the silent plea stolen straight from his heart.

He stared at the metal table, vaguely noticing his blurred reflection in the polished steel. "Listen. Listen, Travis. OK, so you were riding your bike back home from Taft, you were mad because the boys lost and then you were riding past the Pearce farmhouse?" Urgency pounded against James's temple with every beat of his pulse. He had to get Travis to say he was innocent! *Tell me, Travis. Tell me!* he silently screamed. The endless shriek in his head cried for release, words failing him as he contemplated the disaster of a confession.

Travis nodded, and kept nodding. "Yeah. Then it just comes to me. Burn it down. Burn him before he burns you. So I did." He took a puff on the cigarette and eyed James from across the table. "Just like that. No thinkin'. Just snapped and burned it down."

James flinched. The words, the matter-of-fact attitude, stung him like a surprise slap across the face. His heart pounded heavy against his ribs. His blood froze and iced his veins. That cold, dead statement, made in that blunt, no-nonsense tone, shattered his composure and ate away at his certainty that Travis was innocent. Urgency twisted into defeat.

Travis eyed James directly. "I didn't mean for everyone to die."

5

What's done is done, and it can't be undone. Duane's words haunted James as he leaned against his truck in the blinding snow and tried to think of better days—days when his childhood friend wasn't incarcerated for multiple homicides.

Days when this town vibrated with life, when hope rode on people's shoulders and possibilities for the future were bright with promise. Dreams, that's what this town was now missing. The imagination to move forward, the feeling that one could go out and conquer the world with sheer will and determination. The town, the people, were now dark with tragedy, as if everyone waited, breathless, for the next horrible event, no longer sure they had a future at all. His mind and heart revolted against the act that laid waste to people's dreams. *Why, God? Why?* He flung the words mentally towards heaven, the same ones that his hurting parishioners had tossed up to the Lord. Those same parishioners whom he had soothed and assured that that their silent God was truly listening and that beauty would come from ashes. What kind of beauty could come from the ashes of the flesh and bones of this family? James clenched his jaw, the ache forcing his thoughts from whatever answers God might have for him.

Across a frozen baseball field, a group of teens loitered on the aging bleachers. Teasing taunts and occasional laughter carried across the expanse of ground. Watching the young adults—if they could even be called anything remotely close to adults—should have evoked the nostalgia he was seeking; but it didn't. Too much sorrow, confusion, pain coated the years for James to see the sparkle that once shined his life.

Hope and promise didn't shine in these teens, either. They weren't self-assured, they didn't share the exuberance kids usually exhibited—that invincible armor which made them make rash decisions, sometimes brought unthinking courage, and occasionally, fresh ideas that bordered on genius. That bliss and goodness was noticeably absent. Tragedy had touched them, had dampened the joyful purpose of simply being alive and having a future.

James pondered the obvious separation of

cliques—a couple girls bundled up in heavy coats and mittens engaged in one conversation; a couple boys huddled in a separate space, looking awkward, and perhaps slightly judgmental as an obvious "bad boy"—complete with stereotypical sagging jeans and a lit cigarette that curled smoke into the crisp air along with his visible breath—cajoled a girl who was his girlfriend...or maybe not his girlfriend. She didn't appear to be too impressed with his attempts to pull her to her feet and into...an embrace?

But the person who stuck out the most was James's own nephew. Ian sat apart, the sullen look, which James now realized was Ian's trademark, frozen on the boy's face as he huddled into his drab jacket and eyed the other teens. Of all the kids, Ian seemed the most isolated, an invisible wall around him that discouraged anyone from getting near, his personal space blocked off like a mime pretending to be trapped in a box. What secret had Ian closed off? Was it teen angst, the everyday problems that plagued high-schoolers? Was it the girl? No date to the prom? Grades? A sports failure? Or did something deeper ride Ian's conscience...drugs? Alcohol? James shied from the obvious, that mental state of depression that sometimes resulted in teens doing horrible acts, to themselves or others. The child he'd known wasn't capable of it...but that child was grown now, and this Ian was a stranger. And thinking on Travis, and how he'd supposedly changed from the innocent, laughing friend James remembered made him wonder if he'd missed the best years of Ian's life.

Again, it crossed James's mind that he needed to have a talk with his sister's son. Why was Ian so distant, even amongst his peers? That didn't bode well in James's mind. How many teen tragedies had he witnessed or seen in the news about isolated, brooding teens who then chose a deadly path? He didn't want that for any young person, but even more so his nephew. He'd make an effort to get to know Ian, gain his trust, and somehow dig through that reserve to find the nephew he once knew— the nephew who plunged through life with happiness.

Mr. Bad-boy hopped to the top bleacher and balanced on one leg, acting as if he might fall. He laughed and took a huge chug from a bottle of beer that James had only just noticed. Miss I'm-not-impressed-with-you rolled her eyes in such a pronounced gesture that James could see it from across the field...or maybe it was the head turn with upturned nose that gave away her opinion. James wasn't too sure of anything these days.

Shaking the melancholy, James hopped back into the truck...but this time, he didn't forget to solidify that mental note to speak to Ian.

~*~

An old wall radiator groaned as James entered his father's house...not just "his father's house" but *home.* James had grown up in this house, listened to the groans of the radiator all his life. The heat and familiarity warmed him as he stepped around the corner and into the living room. James stopped at the threshold as he pulled off his jacket, just as he had when he'd lived here before. Funny how old habits simply returned. Muscle memory, he supposed. There was comfort in the fact that some things could be remembered without his conscious effort, that they didn't distract from more important things. Like the fleeting memories of his mother, her insistence on him completing chores, making beds, cleaning his room, putting away his clothes, hanging up his jacket.

His father sat in his favorite easy chair. Incandescent glow from the bargain-basement lamp cast an orange hue across the old man's face, but did little else to illuminate the otherwise dark room.

Voices from the TV echoed off faux wood paneling that covered the walls. Cigarette smoke swirled into the lampshade from a half-spent cigarette burning in a glass ashtray. If James wasn't mistaken, that was the ashtray he'd given his father for Christmas back...when was it? James must've been around nine years old. Or maybe eleven. His mother was still alive, anyway.

A glimmer of hope settled inside him; his father hadn't tossed the piece of glass. Maybe the man hadn't completely tossed their relationship, either. "Hey. What you watching?" James asked.

His father leaned over the ashtray and took a long drag off the cigarette. Blowing out smoke, he picked up the remote and pointed it towards the TV. "Nothing." He spoke the one word without ever looking up.

That glimmer of hope dimmed, but James tried to stay positive. Somehow, he had the deep conviction that it was up to him to bring his family out of the pall of hopelessness that seemed to have settled. A silent battle raged in his mind as his soul turned to God, but his intellect denied the thought. James shook off the traitorous heart and firmly shut the door to his thoughts. He smiled a little and leaned against the doorjamb. "Oh, yeah? I hear that's a good show."

Whatever was on TV had Glen Moore's rapt attention. He didn't even an attempt to glance at James. The glimmer fizzled and burned out, replaced by a frustration so complete James struggled to remain civil. His anger at his previous thoughts, the foundering relationship with that Father also upsetting, came out in his words. "All right, look, Dad, I'm sorry I didn't become what you or everybody else had in mind for me—"

"You think that's what's eating me, do you?" his father said, his gaze still glued to the old console TV.

James shrugged. "Isn't it?"

Finally, that question warranted a glance from the old man. "What you do with your life is your business. We all make our own choices."

"OK. Yeah. Fine, right; I buy that. So, why are you so angry with me?"

"Who said I was angry? I'm not angry."

"OK: Disappointed." James let out a heavy sigh. Was his father going to argue semantics instead of getting to the crux of what had formed the chasm between them?

His father pointed the remote control at

the TV, pressed a button—evidently MUTE based on the instant silence which filled the room—and then shifted in the chair a little as he placed his full attention on James.

Finally.

"For no reason you ever explained to me, you run away from here, from me, and from everything that God had planned for you. Now and then you come bouncing back. Most likely when you're running away from something else. And this time you need answers because the road you've been on is so filled with U-turns, you don't know which way it runs."

James shook his head and scrubbed the tension from the back of his neck. "All right. Look, Dad, first of all, I became a minister. I didn't run way from you or anybody else. I had a calling, and it wasn't as sudden as you make it out to be. You know that."

"Fine."

The lone word was meant to placate, not affirm, and James's temper rose a notch. He sucked in a deep breath through his nose. "I didn't come here looking for answers or your sympathy."

"Son, every seed you've planted, everything you've put in the ground—including your mother—hasn't yielded a single thing. And that's not my fault; it's not your mother's fault; and it certainly isn't God's fault.

"My question for you is simple. Do you ever plan on finishing anything?" His father leaned over the ashtray, took a final drag off the cigarette and then ground the butt into the cut glass.

James willed his waning anger to remain burning strong as his dad's words seeped in. Was it true? Was he really a quitter? He stared at his dad for a moment and then shook his head, shook off the man's unjust criticism, shook off his own self-doubt. He wasn't a quitter! Sure he'd moved on a few times, but that wasn't because he'd given up so much as he'd realized where he was, what he was doing at the time just wasn't right.

Like shutting the door to God? James willed his conscience to be quiet, to let him think through the implications of his earthly father's words. Is that how Dad saw him? A failure who ran like a scared rabbit every time something crossed his path that he couldn't control? His mind went back to Dad's words about planting...had any seed he'd planted even grown? He'd been so full of conviction at the beginning of his calling. He was certain that his exhortations hadn't fallen on deaf ears. In the early days, people had come to his church, been baptized, married, and had even specified that he officiate at their funerals. He'd led his flock from birth to death, all in the name of the Lord.

Letting out a puff of frustration, he turned and left his father in the dim glow of the musty living room.

As he hit the front door, muffled voices from the TV filtered down the hall.

James huddled into his coat as he stepped into the snowy night. Moments ago, he'd wallowed in the security of familiar routine, now he had to control the anger that rose. His thoughts were a jumble of memories and frustration, of loss, pain, and now, guilt. Had James abandoned them, had he run away to keep from facing troubles? His father thought the reverent, upstanding minister he'd become, the man who tended his flock with care and patience, was in reality a coward hiding beneath the collar and the cross. The revelation stunned James. He'd known his father didn't seem to approve of his calling, but he'd never realized how deep Glen Moore's disappointment ran.

James muttered to himself as he trudged the deep snow-covered ground to his truck. How dare his dad cast judgment. The man had checked out of James's life years ago. What did he know about James? Nothing!

Lord, help me maintain perspective here.

I know Dad loves me...I think he does...I'm pretty sure he does. Help me to see his side of it. If it's me who needs to change, Lord, then show me where and how. If it's him, Lord, give me the patience to wait.

He climbed into the driver's seat and slammed the blue steel door against the cold. He shook his head as he turned the key in the ignition. What was he thinking? God wasn't listening anymore!

The truck grumbled its own protest as the engine fought to turn over. James dropped into gear and headed out. A nice, quiet drive to clear his head would help. As he hit Kipling's main street, flashing emergency lights set off a beacon outside a run-down house. An ambulance, fire truck, and several police vehicles littered the yard, their lights lighting up the yard and street like a blaze.

James slowed as he approached and parked a few doors down. Spectators formed a human perimeter that mimicked the yellow tape that warned in bold black letters POLICE LINE DO NOT CROSS.

James slowed as he approached and parked a few doors down. Duane was just coming out of the house as James hopped out of the truck and headed to the house. Absently, he noted the teens he'd seen at the ball park earlier, clustered together on the opposite corner from the house. They stood stiff and silent, their demeanor withdrawn and cold, as if they'd drawn into themselves, desperately trying to shield themselves from whatever fresh tragedy encompassed their world.

Duane met James at the police tape. The man looked unusually pale, sick. "Just keeps getting worse," He said, his voice weary.

"What?" James shoved his hands into the pockets of his jacket.

"Looks like a kid blew his brains out with a shotgun in there."

James let out a grunt in disbelief and sadness. He turned and took a look at the cluster of teens. He recognized the one girl...the maybe-girlfriend from earlier, and a couple of the others, but the bad-boy and Ian were both missing. His heart dropped a beat or two as the possibility that "the kid" was Ian crossed his mind. How would he tell his sister? *Please, God*...the soul-wrenching cry from his heart didn't register in his brain at first; it was buried so deep in his psyche, that or several moments, James didn't even notice his heart had turned straight to God.

"It's not pretty."

He turned back to Duane. "Who?"

"Local boy. Drew Abbott. Family moved

here after you were gone. Kid was nothing but trouble from the get-go." He shook his head. "Man!"

One of Duane's deputies walked up and whispered to Duane. "Can't find the kid's mother."

"OK. Get hold of his dad. I think he still works nights over in Deerview...and find his mother."

The deputy nodded and then left.

Duane turned his troubled face back to James.

"Suicide? Why?" James asked.

"I don't know, Jimmy. I don't know. It's a mess in there. The boy was always working me over time. Drunk or drugs, who knows these days. Not the first call I've had about him. Out mouthing, showing off, doing stupid stuff." Duane shrugged. "Like I said, not the same place it was when we were kids. Not by a long shot." He heaved in a heavy breath and let it out. He turned to go back to the house, but then stopped. "Hey Jimmy, if you got one still left in you, say a prayer." He turned and walked away.

Bad as he felt, the only prayer James had left in him was the accidental variety. He couldn't pray for this kid, this town, Duane, or Travis. God simply wasn't listening to James these days, no matter how grave the situation.

And James wasn't partial to wasting his breath.

He stood in the frigid outdoors for only-God-knew how long, until he couldn't feel the end of his nose or the lobes of his ears. Most of the activity had died down. Only on police cruiser remained and most of the crowd had dissipated. Those who were left had formed a tight group, and James could hear them praying to his absentee God. A part of him wanted to join them. A part of him wanted to scream at them so they'd know their pleas were falling on deaf ears. And a part of him cried at the loss of the One who held his heart for so long. Emptiness filled him, followed closely by the bitter, rancid taste of defeat, the soul-sucking silence that used to be filled with love and a passion for life. He couldn't help anyone. He couldn't even help himself. There were no words of comfort he could offer, not with that kid's life snuffed out before the boy really had a chance to live. Who was he to offer platitudes and condolences? He was as drained as rain-parched earth, a desert where everything was withered and dead. That described his heart perfectly, despite its death throes of calling out to his silent God. Bitterness swallowed his anger. It was time to go.

He inched towards his truck but stopped when he reached the teenagers. Ian was among them now, but he just stared at James with contempt and then walked away. The others, somber and speechless eyed him back as if they expected he'd inflict pain or judgment.

He did neither.

6

James opened the door of the old, dilapidated church building and made his way towards the altar. Despite his bitter denial last night, he needed to clear his head. This was the only place he could sort out his thoughts without interruption. He needed to understand, to clarify, to home in on what was happening in this town, with Travis, with Ian and for that matter, with Ian's friend who had ended his life last night. Drew Abbott. What made the boy give up on his life? What was hidden beneath such despair?

The events of last night swirled in his mind, the haunted faces of the teenagers creating a specter in his mind. Duane's weary voice echoed like a harbinger. Ian's distant contempt—or was it something else— hammered panic.

Travis's image formed in clear, 3D color as James recalled this morning's visit. He'd felt compelled to tell Travis of Drew Abbott's suicide, but he hadn't been prepared for

Travis's reaction. Sure, he'd seemed a little stunned by it before his mouth had finally twisted into that odd little smile of his, but that quirky grin was the only normalcy in the conversation.

"Killed himself huh? What he do, jump off a grain elevator, a radio tower? The boy was always lookin' for new heights if you know what I mean."

"Shot himself."

Travis's smile disappeared, and he stared as if it were going to take some time to digest, but then he just shrugged. "Oh. Doesn't surprise me either way. Coulda seen that train wreck coming."

Coulda seen that coming? Travis's words from this morning slammed into focus.

What had Travis been alluding to? Had he seen the boy's despair for what it was? Could Travis, who rarely was able to read people's intentions, have seen beneath this boy's exterior arrogance and understood there was something desperate running deep within the boy's heart? How was that possible? Even professionals had difficulty determining such utter depression without penetrating assessment.

James shook the memory from his mind and dropped to his knees at the altar steps. He gazed up at the familiar image of Jesus. Where had God been while Drew took his own life? Where had God been when Travis decided to head to the Pearce farm? Where was God now? So many people needed Him. James, included. His heart swelled with the loss of his passion, his life, his calling, his God.

He closed his eyes as tears blurred his vision. The moisture seeped from his closed lids, wet his face. "Please, please answer me," he prayed. "I need answers."

A gentle hand touched his shoulder. He looked up with a start.

Pastor John Barrow looked down at James, the same joy-filled expression on his face that James remembered from childhood. "I was told I might find you here," Pastor Barrow said. "We got a new church you know, bricks and stucco. Much warmer than this old place."

James launched himself into the man's embrace. Relief washed over him as he buried his face in Pastor Barrow's neck and accepted the man's welcome. Pastor Barrow's hugs had always inspired comfort. As a young boy and then a troubled, depressed teen, James had often wondered how the pastor's one-armed embraces could feel infinitely more reassuring than his own father's two-armed ones, which so often felt forced and obligatory. Decades later, the consolation in John Barrow's embrace had not diminished.

He pulled away from the pastor's friendly welcome and smiled. His smile remained as he followed the pastor to the new parsonage. Perhaps the newness of the building was a corollary to the renewal of the faith he so desperately needed. His heart clutched at the hope before James had a chance to extinguish it.

They sat opposite each other on separate couches in the sparse but functional living area. A fire crackling from the fireplace and Christmas garland strung across the mantel gave the place warmth.

"So you woke up one day, and try as you might, He just wasn't there, right?" Pastor Barrow asked.

How did he know? Had he experienced his life's higher purpose seeping out, too? This complete withdrawal of all that sustained him, as if a rug had been ripped from beneath his feet? Had Pastor Barrow's soul windmilled, lost and tumbling in a space so vast that the disorientation alone wouldn't allow him to concentrate on anything else? Did all pastors go through it? And the most important question of all…would this relentless, empty vessel, his very soul, ever be filled with God's grace and love again?

James rubbed his forehead in a nervous

gesture that did nothing to calm him or help him focus his thoughts. "Yeah. Something like that. John, I've prayed. I've gone to my knees and begged. I've read and reread the Scriptures until my eyes want to fall off my face, and nothing. No...no answers. Nothing."

"But so many questions." Pastor Barrow's face was kind, open. He waited.

"It just doesn't make sense," James said, looking up at the pastor across the short distance that separated them.

"And what doesn't make sense?"

James shook his head. "Any of it. Anything. Everything. Everything that's happening in the world...this thing with Travis. This terrible thing that he's done. Will s-somebody please explain to me what's going on!" His words came out in a flurry of frustration as his heart pounded hard. His whole body trembled with loss—the loss of his faith, the loss of hope, the loss of his sister's joy, the loss of the town's peace, the loss of the family destroyed by fire, Travis...and now Drew. His poor family.

His temple throbbed, and he grabbed at his forehead. If he could just make sense out of the senseless. "John, every day I look around. Innocent lives are being destroyed. Wars over differences of...faith? And children, sweet young children being taken from us by guns and bullets and brutal acts of nature. And those of us who are supposed to be protecting them, giving them faith, showing them guidance, they commit the most unspeakable acts of all. They all but desecrate His name. Is it any wonder that people are running away from the church, abandoning their faith?" He silenced his rant to take a cleansing breath. His words spoke anger and frustration at the world, but deep down James blamed God. And that knowledge plagued him.

He looked at Pastor Barrow who sat so patiently opposite him, the man's wise gaze both knowing and sympathetic. Shame colored James's thoughts. The good pastor was trying to help him, to act as a confidante, a confessor. Fine. Perhaps talking about it would order his thoughts.

"I know," James said, speaking more calmly now, "that He has a reason, but for the first time in my life, I need to understand here"—he tapped the side of his head—"I need to understand why He would allow such…*terrible* things." He lowered his gaze for a moment as the anguish of what he was about to say choked him before he could utter the words. Slowly he raised his gaze to face the pastor once again. "And, He won't answer me now. When I need Him so desperately, when I've...when I've given my entire life to Him." Emotion clogged his throat and burning tears glazed his vision. "It scares me in ways I can't describe."

He broke down, and the silence stretched through the room.

"James, when you were younger, did I ever tell you the story of my first cat, Freddy, and how I lost my arm?" Pastor Barrow settled in his seat a little, readying himself to tell the story.

James chuckled. "No. I don't think so."

The pastor smiled. "Well, listen carefully. When I was a boy about five years of age, I desperately wanted a little dog, and I picked one out, my mum and I, and we brought it home. But, my dad just about blew a gasket. He stormed at us, 'I don't want to be walking around this house and step in piles of dog poop.' And he ordered us to return the dog immediately. And I was devastated. I was heartbroken.

"And then, about a week later, my mum showed up with a little kitten. She'd convinced my dad that that did not pose the same sanitation problems. Now, he was not thrilled with this, but he was a man of *occasional* reason"—the pastor let out a chuckle—"and a bit of common sense. And I think he also understood that this would teach me a sense of responsibility, by looking after the little thing.

"Anyway, I got my dear, precious little Freddy, and I was thrilled. And less than three months later, he died. Just like that." He snapped his fingers in illustration. "I was so brokenhearted, and do you know what I came up with through all this?"

"What?" James asked.

"There cannot be a God; and if perhaps there was, He was a mean old man—even meaner than my dad. And my dad could cut through granite with his temper and his tongue!"

James waited a beat to hear the rest of the story, but Pastor Barrow just sat there smiling as if waiting for James to catch on.

"Obviously you found your way back," James prompted.

The pastor nodded slowly, knowingly. "Yes, I did. As you will, too, James. Have patience. Have faith. God has not forsaken you."

James smiled at his childhood mentor. His heart beat steady, and the throbbing in his head had gone. Having the opportunity to talk things out really did make a difference. He'd known that as a counselor, but he'd never before had to do it for himself. Just talking with a colleague, who understood on both a personal and a professional level, had helped. His outlook, while not completely restored, had definitely improved. He opened his mouth to thank the pastor, but then remembered something. He eyed Pastor Barrow quizzically. "Wait. Wait a minute; what did that have to do with losing your arm?"

"Nothing, absolutely nothing. I just wanted to make sure that you were listening."

~*~

A smile still curled the edges of James's mouth as he drove across the frozen road into town. Dusk had set in early, and the dim, grey light coaxed bleak thoughts. Pastor Barrow's words ran through his mind. *God has not forsaken you.* Maybe that was true, but it sure felt as though He had. And again, what about Travis? Had God forsaken him, too? A man so innocent of mind, yet now seemingly guilty of unspeakable violence. James had sinned greatly in his life, if not in deed, then in thought. It was logical that God would turn away from that. But Travis? Travis—until the fire, evidently— hadn't had a bad thought or done a bad thing to anyone. How could God have let him go?

It didn't add up.

James pulled into the diner parking lot and then headed inside for a meal. He supposed he should go home, check in with his sister. She had told him they'd normally be eating dinner about now, but he just wanted to be alone to sort things out in his mind without subjecting anyone else to his clouded mind and inconstant mood. From high to low, from doubt and fear to laughter and being uplifted, his mind was a mess of roiling emotions which he'd still not sorted out, despite talking to Pastor Barrow. Uncertainty dogged his thoughts, his heart and mind warring with each other as they tried to still the troubled waters within.

The warmth inside the diner was punctuated by Christmas music tinkling in the background from the overhead speakers. Quiet chatter joined the chorus from the few occupied tables. He took note of the table of teenagers in the back corner as he took a seat a few booths and a row over. He recognized the one girl from the ball park...and the suicide house. James let out a deep breath wrought with sadness, and then he smiled at Loretta, and ordered steak and potatoes without looking at the menu. He might not know much these days, but at least he knew what he wanted for dinner.

Before he realized any time had passed, Loretta set a plate in front of him. Absently, he nodded his thanks before silently thanking God for the food. There it was again...that old habit that evidently did die hard. Maybe the pastor was right. Maybe God hadn't forsaken James, and maybe deep down James knew it. Why else would he keep speaking to the invisible and non-existent Being?

Faltering faith. It was not a situation that had ever crossed his mind in the early days. Oh, sure, he had a few moments of being a doubting Thomas, despite the miracles he'd witnessed when the Lord stepped into someone's life, but he never thought he'd be in a position to deny the God he served. But the silence in his heart was deafening...so deafening that it had obliterated the very passion that had sustained him all these years. *Where are You, God? Why have You forsaken me?* But he wasn't here to worry about his troubles, not really. He was here to sort out Travis's problems, and maybe make peace with his dad, with the town, and then start his own new life.

He glanced over his shoulder at the group of teens huddled at the table in the corner. Their low voices and sullen faces reminded him so much of Ian. Was there something in the water in Kipling, these days, or was it everywhere?

Brooding seemed to be synonymous with teenager. He'd been emotionally withdrawn at that age, too, but he'd always assumed it was because of the death of his mother. Surely not *every* teen in Kipling had endured such loss.

The fire. Oh, right: The fire had affected the town in its entirety. And this group had also lost one of their own in a violent way. Still...

"D'you want me to stick that in the microwave for you? Gotta be colder than the cow that died for it by now," Loretta said.

"Nah, thanks...Hey"—James motioned with his head to the corner booth—"the girl back there wearing the beret, who is she?"

Loretta glanced over. "That's Amanda Spencer. She was Drew Abbott's girlfriend, or whatever they call it these days." She gave an empathetic shrug, and then adjusted the Santa hat on her head. "She hasn't always been this way. She kinda flew off the rails. A lot of them do." Dangling Santa Claus earrings swayed with the shake of her head. "You know, there's nothing really here for them, no way out..." she broke off and let out a heavy sigh. "And then what Drew did..."

James twisted in the booth to take a better look at the girl he'd first seen on the bleachers. What made a young girl fly off the rails? What caused a young boy to kill himself? It seemed a contradiction that in a town where there was nothing for teens to do, they'd find reasons to fly off the rails. In his day, they'd painted the town's water tower in the school colors, worn masks and driven an unmarked tractor through the gym. That had certainly caused a ruckus, but no one was hurt. Of course, tragedy caused reactions like suicide. The lure of excitement also caused such reactions, but in the middle of small town living, what other lure could there be? Teens rebelling against their parents' rules, committing suicide, out of boredom? There had to be more to it than that.

Or was James just too old to catch a clue?

He turned back to Loretta and then glanced at his plate. She was right; the food was cold. "Yeah," he said and handed her the plate. "Maybe you should. Thank you."

As she went to warm his meal, he turned his attention once again to the table in the corner. This time, Amanda Spencer was looking at him. He wondered if the contempt reflected in her face was directed towards him or something else. In her own way, was she trying to reach out, using that arrogant façade to let him know she desperately needed to talk to someone and hoping she'd not have to take the first step? He'd counseled many a teen, but they were young Christians who didn't have to deal with a boyfriend's suicide, or worry about losing their popularity because of it. How many of her friends secretly thought she was the cause of Drew's despair? How many thought maybe she was a mean girl, or pregnant, or did something else to make him take his own life?

He decided that when he talked to Ian, he'd try to subtly ask about Amanda. Maybe he could help. Or not. Without God, maybe he couldn't help anyone anymore. His calling was gone. Perhaps his life was meant to go in a completely different direction. *The ball is back in Your court, God.*

He cleared his mind of contemplating the facets of teenage angst and his own shortcomings, and instead focused on Travis. Regardless of Travis's confession, James still didn't believe the man was guilty. The Travis he'd known practically from birth, whom he'd grown up with, didn't have a mean bone in his body.

As he finished his meal and headed home, James went over everything Travis had told him. If he thought on it long enough, hard enough, he'd get to the bottom of it. There was a flaw in something Travis said, and James would find it, pursue it, and convince Duane that the whole matter needed to be looked over once again. He expected that last task to be the most difficult.

The house was dark and quiet when he arrived. He sneaked down the hallway to his bedroom, changed into pajamas, and climbed between the sheets. His mind was still spinning with images and recollections of conversation as he slipped to sleep.

Heat seared the air. Flames roared like an agitated lion ready to devour anyone who came close, and licked the sky in plumes of black smoke and orange tendrils.

"What's done is done and can't be undone." Duane's voice rose above the rumbling flames.

Travis materialized through the smoke, the burning cherry of his cigarette looming close. "Burn it down. Burn him before he burns you."

Travis dissolved into the disappointed face of Glen Moore. "Do you ever plan on finishing anything?"

James ran, ran from the taunts, from the heat, from the flames that threatened to torch his life.

He let out a loud scream and suddenly…

He was awake. Focusing to calm his racing heartbeat, James took deep, deliberate breaths. Sweat-soaked pajamas clung to his body as he tried to escape the bedding wound around his legs and waist. Flames still feathered in his thoughts, wisps of memory tangling with his emotions, a chaotic quagmire of pain and loss overriding his physical world. It took a few seconds in the darkened room to calm down.

It was dream. Only a dream.

7

James trudged through the shin-deep snow towards the remains of the Pearce farm. His breath preceded him in visible puffs as if guiding him. Moving pieces of debris, he looked for any clue that might help him understand what had happened that fateful night.

Nothing.

He couldn't even see why they'd deemed it arson. Then again, he wasn't an arson investigator, so he had no idea what clued them into declaring it such.

Moving around the property from what was left of the house's foundation, he stopped for a moment at the swing set. Absently he pushed the two-seater air glider. The Pearce children had been teenagers. What had they thought of this swing set? Had they flounced out here in teenaged angst to sit in the swing while they pouted away whatever had rocked their world for the moment? Had they sat out here in twilight, content with their lives, giddy with the excitement of being young? Perhaps even in love? How long had Mary said the Pearces had lived in Kipling? Five years? So the kids had been maybe ten years old when they'd arrived. Probably on the cusp between loving this swing set and thinking they were too old for it.

Had Mr. Pearce installed the toy or was it already here when they bought the farm? Bought the farm. James grunted at his choice of words and the tragic, but apropos, accidental play on words.

He shook inconsequential thoughts from his head and made his way through the snow back to what once was a house. He ran a finger along the charred edge of cinderblock as he walked the perimeter of the house hoping to find a shard of evidence that would exonerate Travis. He reached down and moved a fallen and fragile tree limb, and found something poking out of the snow.

A book. He reached down and plucked it from the ground, dusted snowflakes from the cover. The white leather was soiled from dirt and soot, but surprisingly, only the edges of the cover were charred beyond repair. Gold gilt letters proclaimed the book a Holy Bible.

His heart jolted.

Carefully pulling back the cover, James

revealed onionskin paper, untouched completely by the fire. Yet, he'd found it at the foundation of the house. Even the cinderblock had burned. But not God's Word.

Therefore, we who are receiving the unshakable kingdom should have gratitude, with which we should offer worship pleasing to God in reverence and awe. For our God is a consuming fire. The words from Hebrews chapter twelve struck him. God is a consuming fire, His kingdom, unshakeable, even in the midst of human fire—which cannot destroy He Who is an all-consuming fire.

Or His everlasting Word. *Offer worship…in reverence and awe.* When was the last time James had offered reverence? Awe? He'd offered obedience, he'd offered time—even money—but how long had it been since he'd truly allowed himself to be awed by the wonder and beauty of God? For that matter, when had he offered even the slightest gratitude for the gifts God had given him—not just the *thanks be to God* lip service, but the thought-out, humble, thank You for my athletic successes, family and friends, a vocation to preach, and the congregation to hear the words preached.

Or for his father, who had worked long hours all his life to provide a home for James and Mary, even if the man wasn't loving, forgiving, or understanding.

When had he traded that goodness for a mud puddle of self-pity and doubt?

About the same time you stopped hearing My Voice.

James staggered back at the revelation, almost losing his grip on the Bible.

Was it possible it wasn't that God had stopped talking, but rather that James had stopped listening? His heart jolted again. Shock colored his thoughts now.

Well, from here out, no more self-pity. No more whining. He was going to prove Travis's innocence and then forge ahead with his own life, no matter where that journey might lead. *OK, God?* he asked tentatively as he stood in snow that had just begun to fall steadily. A slight breeze whistled through the expanse of space. James held his breath. *OK, God?* he asked again, trying to make his inner voice sound firmer.

No answer.

James clenched his jaw in frustration and the sudden urge to give up. Instead of focusing on it, he tucked the Bible into his jacket pocket and made his way to his truck. He couldn't lose the reverence for God's Word, despite God's silence.

~*~

James swung open the restaurant door to let in his sister, Abby, and Ian. He looked back at his father who waved him through with a gesture that said: Don't wait for me; I can take care of myself. His father, ever the independent, I-don't-need-you type.

James shrugged and followed his sister into the building. There were days when he was just done trying to reach his father, but then, there were days when it seemed he spent every waking hour trying to connect. Both his earthly father and his Heavenly Father seemed as distant as ever, and James wondered why he worked so hard when neither seemed interested in maintaining the relationship.

"Daddy!" Abigail squealed and headed towards a buffet table across the room.

Rick, Mary's ex-husband, looked up and gave his daughter a huge grin and then scooped her into a hug.

"Let's go." The blunt order came from his father. James looked back and then to Mary.

"It's OK, Dad. He has a right to be here."

"I'll be in the car." Glen Moore turned and left, his face as stony as granite and his posture as stiff as the expression on his face.

Tension tightened across James's neck.

Didn't his dad understand that when he rejected Rick, it hurt Mary and the kids? She had enough raising two children without Dad censuring her. Especially in public.

"Dad—" Mary started, but broke off as the door shut behind their father.

Rick, carrying Abby, walked up to Ian and patted him on the shoulder. "Son," he acknowledged before extending a hand to James. "Hey, Jim. Heard you were around."

James tentatively shook Rick's hand as he took note that Ian had ignored his dad. James wanted to be civil, but he didn't want to betray his sister, either. "Yeah. It's been a while," he said. The man was either a supremely good actor or he was clueless about the tension he'd caused. James glanced back at Mary.

Her attention was on the closed glass door. "Maybe we better go."

"Why, Mommy?" Abby asked.

Rick brightened. "She's right. Go get your ol' man and let's put a couple tables together." He glanced over his shoulder.

James followed Rick's gaze to a young brunette who was standing at the buffet table. She smiled, but the gesture didn't travel to her eyes.

"He's already in the car," Mary said flatly. "He won't come back in. Maybe another time."

"All right." Rick set Abigail on her feet. "Just trying to be civil about this."

"Maybe another time."

"Yeah, you said that." Rick sighed and then looked to James. "Jimmy, let's catch up. Mary knows where to find me."

"Sounds like a plan," James replied noncommittally. The tension in his neck throbbed. "I-I'll give you a call." He hoped Rick didn't mean it. He really didn't want to go over the ashes of a dead relationship with this man, despite Rick's children being James's niece and nephew. James glanced one more time at the brunette across the room and then ushered Abby to the door.

Mary and Ian followed close behind.

James wondered where they were going to grab a bite now before the Christmas pageant got underway. Norm's had the best Christmas buffet in town.

They piled back in to Mary's car, and she started the engine.

"What was all that about, Dad?" James asked.

"Never you mind about that." He twisted in the passenger seat to glance back at the kids sitting next to James. "I was just thinking, we might want to get supper after the pageant." He sneered slightly at James. "You spent so much time in there yammerin' with that man that there isn't a whole lot of time for eatin' now."

"We could've stayed. Mary didn't mind," James countered, suddenly feeling as defensive as a chastised teenager. He looked across the front seat at Mary. She didn't look back, but he caught the almost imperceptible shake of her head.

OK, so she didn't want to press the matter. If she didn't care, then he didn't care, either. He settled back in the seat and put his arm around Abigail. "You excited to sing, sweetheart?"

Her face split into a wide grin and soft curls bobbed across her shoulders as she nodded emphatically. "It's so fun, Uncle Jimmy! I get to be in the front row."

"That's fantastic, Abigail...I mean, Abby. I can't wait to see it."

Her enthusiasm was refreshing, but caused a twinge of melancholy. He'd missed out on so much of his family's lives by being gone. Maybe a decision to stay home for good would be the right thing to do. He'd thought as much several times over the last few days, so maybe this was where God wanted him.

"Don't forget your bag, Abby," Mary reminded as she pulled into the parking spot at the auditorium. "Let's get you changed into your pageant outfit."

As they walked into the lobby, James spotted Rick across the way. Rick eyed him and waved.

A grunt from behind heralded the moment his father spotted Mary's ex-husband.

"Be nice, Dad," Mary said softly. "C'mon, Abby. Let's get you ready." Mary ushered Abby down the curved corridor to the back of the main stage.

"Can I just go?" Ian mumbled.

"Yeah," James's father said. "With me. Into the auditorium. And no complaining. Don't you know it's Christmas?" He gave Ian a tug on the arm and led him through the open double doors on the other side of the common area.

His family took dysfunction to a new level, James thought.

Rick approached, and James greeted him with a chin nod.

"How'd you get here so fast?"

"We kind of lost our appetites after…well, you know: *after*." He shrugged. "We'll eat later." He motioned to the empty corridor that led to the vending display. "Wanna talk?"

James nodded. "Sure."

"You know, this gal I'm seeing, the one at Norm's—I know what that looks like. Half my age. I know what I'm going through. I'm not stupid; I'm reacting. It's a cliché, but you know what? It feels good. She makes me feel good about myself, and with all due respect to your sister, that's something I went without for a long time."

"I'm sorry to hear that." James didn't believe it for a minute. Mary had her faults, but it took two to make a marriage, and Rick, despite being here for Abby's pageant, seemed as oblivious as a rock. He'd barely said two words to Ian.

"When you left here Mary was fourteen. Your mother wasn't in the ground six months. Now I'm not here to blame you or anyone, but your little sister was left to play daughter, mother, friend, and everything in between. And your dad was hurting. Bad. And the worse he got, the harder she tried. And in all these years, nothing has changed. He's still angry, and she's still trying to make him happy." He paused and looked James square in the eye. "I couldn't compete with that anymore."

Noise from the main entrance drew James's attention. He turned as a crowd entered the lobby and headed into the main theater. James was grateful for the distraction; he wasn't sure how to respond to Rick. He wanted to understand the man's point of view—as a

Christian and a pastor, he should be able to turn the other cheek, be understanding—but Rick had walked out on Mary and the kids and taken up with another woman. Maybe Mary had been overly-attuned to their father's needs, but was that a reason to abandon her? Honor your father and mother ran deep in James's soul, and he was certain Mary had just as deep a commitment to their parents. Leaving her to pick up the broken pieces of all their hearts wasn't fair.

Isn't that what you did? James ignored the silent accusation that paraded through his mind. He hadn't abandoned his sister; he'd grown up and moved away. That was a normal process of maturation, not a shirking of responsibility. He'd had a calling and a job. It was only right to take it.

He nodded towards the crowd, cueing Rick that it was time make their way back.

The main theater was already humming with conversation. It looked as though most of the town had turned out. James scanned the crowd and found his dad and Ian seated stage right and midway down the tiered rows.

The band finished playing an introduction as a young woman walked center stage to introduce the choir. The children filed out in rows, all looking festive and uniformed in black bottoms and white tops adorned with a single red Christmas bow edged in gold. They centered themselves on stage between two decorated Christmas trees and near-to-life-sized lighted ornaments of Santa, a snowman, and a candle.

The lone boy in the group—sans Christmas bow, but plus red bowtie—looked slightly uncomfortable surrounded by twenty-plus girls, and James had to smile. One day, that kid would thrill to be surrounded by so many females!

Cued and ready, the band played the opening strains of "Silent Night" and the choir began to sing. The lovely tune and the joyous words lifted to the rafters, the children's voices blending to bring meaning that transcended their surroundings. They did pretty well for a group of young amateurs, their combined voices almost angelic. An automatic smile lifted James's mouth. He watched his family from a distance, grateful for the moment to observe without interaction. He father was also smiling...actually *smiling*. The sight both warmed James and emphasized how little joy he saw in his father these days—years, for that matter. Losing their mother had profoundly changed him. James missed his dad, the one from before his mother's death. His gaze traveled to his nephew.

Ian sat, still stoic and broody, huddled into his jacket as if it were cold in the auditorium.

It wasn't.

Something wasn't right with Ian. James touched on several things that could cause Ian that much angst, but nothing came to mind. Had the divorce affected him more than they knew? But Mary wasn't oblivious to them at all. Despite the silences at meals, she was attentive with an ease that spoke of not only practice, but also that told him she didn't miss the subtle nuances and details of her children's needs. And it couldn't be Drew's death, because Ian had been broody and silent before Drew passed. The scene at the bleachers came to mind. James dismissed his concerns, determined to talk to Ian as soon as possible.

From front row, center stage, Abby caught Rick's eye. He waved at her, pride beaming from his face. She grinned and waved back, then adjusted the battery-operated candle she was holding in tandem with the rest of the choir.

This was the Abby who James remembered, a pretty little girl, anxious to please, thrilled to show off her new skills, and confident that she was loved by her family.

The song ended to thunderous applause, and Abby beamed as she filed off stage with the others.

The rest of the pageant went on, but James found himself preoccupied with his conversation with Rick. James had always assumed the other woman had come before the divorce. Now he wasn't so sure. And what about Mary? Did he deserve part of the blame for her broken marriage? He had left her to deal with his father when she was younger than Ian was now. Logically, he realized he had no control over Mary's—or Rick's—choices, but if he hadn't left her alone with his emotionally stunted father, would she have been better equipped in her marriage—or at least better able to focus on her husband and children instead of tending to the crusty old man their old man had become? Another thought entered his head. Had his mother's death, his father's brooding silence and grief, and his own leave-taking, forced Mary into the arms of someone not suitable, just to get away from the sorrow and pain? Had she not chosen wisely, thinking anything was better than the cold house that had lost the warmth and lifeblood of his mother?

He shook his head. He couldn't be responsible for Mary, for Travis, for his dad, for the whole of Kipling.

He just couldn't.

~*~

Cedar popped in the fireplace, and Abby stirred in James's arms. He adjusted his hold on her and stroked her hair until she settled back to sleep in his lap. It had been a long time since he'd cuddled Abby, and he was enjoying the warmth of her tiny body snuggled close, her absolute trust in his love so humbling. Abby was one of the few people in Kipling who still showed the joy of simply being alive.

Mary walked up to the threshold and stopped, watching him with a satisfied grin on her face. He smiled back and motioned her to join him on the couch.

"Ian OK?" he asked.

"Oh, you know boys," she said and sank onto the sofa beside him. "He's going though that silent stage, marking his territory, but he still needs to know Mommy cares."

"What happened to him, Mary? He seems so withdrawn. Is it the divorce?"

She shook her head. "I don't think so. Sure, Rick's leaving affected him—Abby, too— but they both adjusted to that pretty quickly. Or, at least, seemed to. This...this new thing's been since…" her voice trailed off, and she focused on the twinkling lights of the Christmas tree as though pondering how to choose her words.

James waited watching the soft glow on her face fade from red to blue to green to white with the cycle of the tree light. He reached over and patted her arm. "Since when, Mary?"

"The fire." She raised her gaze to meet his. "I told you it hit everyone hard, but Ian seemed to take it especially hard." She inhaled a deep breath and then released it. "I don't know why. He and the Pearce boy were friends. A bunch of 'em hung out together. You know how teens are. And at times I thought he might be sweet on the girl." She tittered softly. "Not that I want to think about that! He's still just a boy in my mind."

James chuckled briefly then sobered. "I'm sensing a 'but'."

She lifted her eyebrows. "But, the loss seemed to break him more than I think it should. It was tragic, Jimmy, I told you, but for a while there, Ian had nightmares every night. That's why I check on him each night. And then for months he recoiled any time someone lit a cigarette.

"I know they say Travis started the fire with a cigarette, but it's not as if Ian was there to see it. Yet, you should've seen him around Dad—flinching at the sound of a lighter, goin' back and stubbing out butts from the ashtray as though he thought they'd spring back to life and start a fire."

"Did you talk to him about it? Maybe have him see a grief counselor. "

Mary shook her head. "He won't hear of it. Says he's fine. I'm worried about him, Jimmy, but I can't force him into therapy. It wouldn't do any good if he's not willing to let go of whatever it is that's bothering him."

James carefully shifted in the seat, so he could face his sister a little better. Abby stirred, but remained asleep. Her little head lolled against his chest, and she snuggled close, right under his heart. Love suffused him again, that this tiny, fragile creature was part of his family.

"D'you want me to take her?" Mary motioned to Abby.

"No, she's fine. She's a sweetheart."

"D'you want a cup of coffee?"

"I'm good." James wondered if his sister was trying to be hospitable or if her change of subject was an avoidance tack. "So what happened with you and Rick? Was it the woman at the restaurant?" If Mary didn't want to talk about the divorce, she could tell James so, outright.

"No. That came after...or at least I think so."

"So what happened?"

"Truth? It doesn't matter. He and I aren't meant to be together. I thought having Abby—our little mid-life surprise—might be the glue, but...I'm OK. Actually, I'm happier. Ricky's a good dad and that's all that's important. Besides, it's better the kids see us apart and happy than miserable together."

Rick's words resonated in James's mind. They hadn't been happy in a long time... Mary had focused so much energy on their father. He had to ask the question. "Mary, do you hold it against me that I left?"

"What are you talking about?"

"You were just a kid, and I left you to deal with dad...everything. Do you hold that against me? I mean you have every right. I was so selfish."

"Yes, you were, but you were also hurting, and I knew that. To everyone around here you were a hero, but I saw what was going on."

"How can I fix that?"

"You can't. But it's not important. What *is* important to me is that you're here now and you find some peace." She patted his arm in a comforting gesture that had a humbling effect.

She motioned for Abby, and he gently handed off his niece.

As he watched Mary carry Abby down the hallway, he thanked God for his family—whether his words were heard or not. There were still miles to go on the road to reconciliation with his father, but James literally had the most caring sister in the world. Mary was like their mother, nurturing, kind, and willing to set her needs aside to meet others until they figured it all out. She gave people the gift of time, while she continued being the woman God meant her to be. It was a humbling realization, the second moment of humbleness that James had felt this evening.

8

The crowd roared as Duane's son, Carter, led the team down the ice. With seconds to go, Carter slapped in the winning goal. Cheers exploded both in and out of the hockey rink. James and his dad jumped up with the rest of the crowd, clapping and cheering like mad.

"He's good!" his dad said.

"Real good. Better than I ever was."

"Not that good!" His dad eyed him soberly for a moment then grinned and rejoined the cheering.

James almost staggered at his father's moment of connection. A breakthrough, finally. Maybe they could salvage something after all.

Down on the ice, the team jumped all over Carter and exchanged high-fives as the crowd began to file from the risers.

As James and his dad headed out the door, Duane hailed James.

James looked back and Duane held up a hand.

"Uh, Dad, I'll meet you back in the truck,"

James said, patting his dad on the back. He turned and made his way upstream through the exiting crowd as Duane met him halfway.

Duane leaned in so he could be heard above the bustling crowd that surrounded them. "Listen, thought you might want to know; they're gonna be moving Travis. I guess whatever's gonna happen next is setting up to happen before the year's out."

"When? Where?"

"I don't know. That's all I know. Sorry." He nodded, gave James a quick tap on the shoulder, and then turned to leave.

James stood, frozen in place for a moment which the crowd buzzed around him. What would happen to Travis now? Who in this town would visit him if he was moved further away? Not that many did anyway. In fact, James wasn't sure anyone even cared. He went numb inside. He'd failed Kipling once, failed God in His special call; he would not fail Travis. Not this time.

He hoped.

He joined the crowed and filed out of the stadium. The cold air struck his lungs as he crossed the parking lot to the truck. The temperature seemed to have dropped considerably since they'd entered the stadium at the start of the game. Or, maybe it was just the shock and numbness inside that made the cold seem colder. The hinges on the truck squeaked and rattled as he pulled open the door. He hurried into the seat and slammed the door.

"What did Duane want?" his dad asked.

"Oh, nothing." James blew on his hands and rubbed them together.

"Oh yeah, I hear that's a good show." He pulled off his glasses and gave James a pointed look. First in the stadium, and now this. Was his dad actually joking around with him? That tenuous connection forged another link in the chain of reconciliation.

James half-smiled at getting his own words playfully thrown back in his face. "Travis."

"What about him?"

"I don't know. What's your take on all this? You think he could have done what they're saying?" He eyed his dad's weathered face, a face that looked as though it held a host of wisdom. Today, after sharing a hockey match that brought fond memories of bonding and camaraderie, James hoped Glen Moore had copious wisdom to unload. Since his Heavenly Father wasn't imparting much these days, perhaps his earthly one would make a good surrogate. And maybe that connection would grow even stronger, and he and his dad could mend the relationship that broke when his mother died.

"What I think doesn't matter, but isn't Travis saying the same thing—that he did it? I thought this mess was over and done."

"Yeah." Trouble swirled in James's mind as he mentally tried to make sense of the entire situation—now with time running out for Travis. He scrambled to think of a way to save the man, but he had so little to go on. Searching the rubble, digging through the ashes had gleaned only the Word of God. Talking to Travis was like talking to a brick wall. He stoically said he did it with a cigarette, even gave a motive, but beyond that, nothing. No details, no other feelings, no contemplation of the heinous crime's results. That wasn't like Travis, he was always worried about how other people felt. James's thoughts circled. It was hopeless.

Long moments of silence passed between James and his dad, and in an attempt to clear his jumbled thoughts, James focused on low-volume engine revs and human conversations which filtered through the windows.

"You know, I don't go sticking my nose in anyone's manure, but if you're asking if it feels like a square peg is being forced in a round hole, well…"

"So wait…you *don't* think he did it?" That surprise had James reeling. He'd felt so alone in his conviction that Travis was innocent and to find an unlikely ally in his father both shocked him and sparked an ember of hope. Could that hope be fanned into a full-fledged relationship with his father?

"I didn't say that," his dad was quick to say. "I said I don't get involved in stuff like this. I will tell you this however: there's a seed of truth in every lie. What that seed is, what becomes of it—the lie, the official story—that's all up to the guy pulling the plow." He slipped his glasses on his nose and stared out the windshield.

Had his dad tried to fathom the same things James did? That Travis, who had never even contemplated hurting a fly, that in a fit of anger, he'd intentionally let others die? His dad had watched Travis grow up, too. James's thoughts sobered.

The conversation was over, but not James's quest. If the cynical and opinionated Glen Moore thought Travis was innocent, then James was going to find out why Travis would willingly take the fall. *Why would he do that, Lord?* There was no ready or reasonable explanation…unless it was his mother. James could see Travis protecting his mother in such a way.

But then, he could neither see Mrs. Wexler starting the fire or getting away in the time it took for the fire department to arrive. Besides, did Mrs. Wexler still smoke?

Oh, c'mon, James. Mrs. Wexler did not do it.

Who else would Travis protect? The questions screamed through the halls of James's mind. And with each new question came a new frustration.

But he would get to the bottom of it. He wouldn't give up until he did.

Do you ever plan on finishing anything?

James snapped his attention to his father sitting beside him in the truck. The echo of the man's words had been so loud that for a moment, James had thought the man had spoken them again.

His father merely glanced at him and then turned to gaze out the passenger window.

"I'm gonna finish *this*."

"Huh?" His father turned back to him.

"Nothing, Dad. It's nothing."

~*~

James's frustration had not dissipated

much by the time Travis walked into the visiting room at the Bishop Psychiatric Facility. The guard—or orderly, or whatever they were called—closed the door to the stark room.

Travis gave James a curious smile and started to sit at the table.

James did not return the greeting. He was done tiptoeing around the issues. He was determined to get satisfactory answers whether Travis wanted to give them, or not.

"You didn't do it, did you Travis?" The words came out a little harsher than James had intended, but maybe that was a good thing. Direct confrontation had always made Travis nervous.

Travis stood. A tentativeness shone in his eyes that James recognized from bygone days. The high-pitched screech of the chair legs scraping across the concrete floor bounced off the walls as Travis pushed the chair back under the table. His gaze flicked to James, then the wall, then back again to James.

"I don't buy it, Travis. I'm sorry, but I just don't buy it, any of it—the whole story." James kept his tone firm and hoped his expression invited a total confession. He narrowed his eyes a little, trying to be intimidating.

"Me neither. I don't buy your story and what's going on with you. How 'bout that?"

The fire in Travis's tone startled James, but only for a moment. He hadn't expected Travis to turn the tables, but that profound gift had popped out at just the right time. James would not bow to it today, though. He met Travis's gaze directly. "This isn't about me!"

"Oh yeah? Maybe this is *all* about you, Jimmy. "How 'bout that!" Travis shot back, his conviction totally convincing.

"Would you stop!"

"*You* stop!" Travis countered, thrusting an accusing finger towards James. "You started it."

James forced his tone to calm. "Aren't you worried about what's going to happen to you in here? What's going to happen to your mother?"

"She'll be fine. I'll be fine, too. God has His plan. You should know that better than anyone."

James stared, speechless. Travis had a point.

James had to concede that Travis had always been a prophet of sorts. The revelation startled him. God always blessed the innocent. Travis lived his calling. James shook off the thought, making a mental note to ponder later.

"Championship game against Fairmont, you busted your pinky when that tub of lard, Puckett, crushed you. Remember that?"

James smiled faintly and nodded,

wonderment still sizzling along his nerve endings.

"Yeah, that's right. We were five yards from the end zone. Next play, if you didn't get hurt, what play were you gonna call to take the ball in?"

"Pass to Tyler," James replied.

"That's right. But you couldn't throw, so what did you do?"

"Faked the pass, handoff to Clay."

"Touchdown!" Travis slapped the table for emphasis, and the sound echoed through the room. He let out a deep breath. "It's not ours to question His plan, Jimmy. Just to play the game."

9

James hammered on the front door of the Wexler residence. Travis's mother didn't answer the door. "Ms. Wexler?"

"Go away! Leave me alone!" she yelled from inside.

He stepped off the front porch and headed around to knock on the back door. "Ms. Wexler? It's Jimmy Moore. I'd really like to talk to you, ma'am."

No answer.

He rapped on the window in quick succession and finally, Travis's mom swung open the door.

"What do you want?" She barked as she drew her terrycloth robe closer around her body. Years and a few extra pounds had aged her face, but evidently, neither had diminished her sass.

"It's me, ma'am. It's Jimmy Moore."

"I know who you are," she said, with no less causticness than had been in her first words. "You got old. And bald."

James faintly smiled at the blunt statement of the obvious. "Yes, ma'am, well the Lord giveth—"

"And He can snatch it right back from you!" she finished.

"Yes, ma'am. Look, I'd like to talk to you about Travis."

"There's nothing to talk about."

The starkness reflected in her eyes gave James momentary pause. It was as if looking at a stranger, a shell, despite the pluck in her words. Yet, he'd grown up at this house. Spent countless hours here with Travis. He knew this woman. She was practically family. "Do you think maybe we could go inside? We could sit down. Maybe I can take you and we could get a cup of coffee."

"I don't need coffee, and I don't need conversation. Travis is gone, and everyone's happy. Fine!"

"Not me," James said quietly.

"Not you?" The surprise in her voice saddened him. Of all people, she should have believed he'd stand by Travis.

"No ma'am. I'm not happy."

"And why's that?" The surprise in her tone turned to skepticism.

"Gut feeling."

She outright laughed! James began to

smile, too, but then her laugh turned into a cough, chesty and harsh: a smoker's cough.

Had she started the fire? As soon as the absurd thought resurfaced, James tamped it down.

With her mouth covered, she turned and jogged into to the house.

"Ma'am, you all right?" James said.

"Come in. Shut the door!" she hollered from inside. She poured a glass of water and drank it. Then, as he made his way into the kitchen, she turned to face him. She shook her head. "Don't take up smoking."

"Yes, ma'am."

"And stop with all the ma'am business, would you? We're both too old for that."

James grinned. "OK."

She leaned against the counter. "Travis didn't do what he's being blamed for; plain and simple. I know it. You know it."

"You know this as a fact?"

"I know this as a mother," she said without hesitation.

"OK, well then, who did do it?"

She raised her eyebrows and gave him the same pointed look that made him squirm when he was a kid.

"You're suggesting there is someone. What makes you think that?"

"Because everybody—"

"Yeah! Right."

"OK. I see where you're going with this. Let's say there's another explanation for this. Then, why is Travis doing what he's doing? Taking the blame. Why is he saying that he did it? It makes no sense."

"No, it doesn't," she agreed. "But it's Travis we're talking about here. Half of whatever he did in his life never made sense." She paused as if allowing her words to sink in. "But the other half made *perfect* sense."

The weight of her words hit James like a mallet to the gut. Travis wasn't wily enough to harbor ulterior motives. He had a reason for confessing, and once again, James rationalized that the reason had to be protection. But if Travis wasn't protecting his mother, who was he protecting? Who else did Travis care about enough to forfeit the rest of his life to prison?

Everyone. The word was Divine inspiration; James sensed it. But it wasn't useful. Everyone was completely too broad. How would James narrow down *everyone?* He nodded to Ms. Wexler, and as he left her, he promised he'd do whatever he could to prove Travis's innocence.

~*~

125

Sunlight penetrated the clouds as James made his way to the courthouse, and melting snow glistened off the wet asphalt. James lowered the truck's visor to help dissipate some of the glare.

The courthouse parking lot was full; it took him a good five minutes to find a parking spot. He wondered absently what so many people needed with the legal system this close to Christmas.

He entered the stark, grey cinderblock building and made his way to the Office of the Public Defender. James approached the makeshift window, but the clerk did not look up from her task. James leaned over. "Hi."

The woman finished what she was doing before looking at him.

"Hi, yeah," he said. "How would I find the lawyer assigned to a particular case?"

"What case?"

"Travis Wexler. He was involved in—"

"That's Paula Roggin."

"And how would I find her?"

"Who are you?" The clerk gave him a skeptical look.

"Friend of the defendant."

The clerk seemed to relax a little. "Well, it's your lucky day." She glanced behind him, her gaze travelling as she pointed.

James turned just as a woman bustled past him, her briefcase poised, her suit plain. "Thank you," James said to the clerk before hurrying to catch up with the public defender.

"Paula, there's somebody to see you," the clerk said as Paula Roggin arrived at her desk.

James approached.

"Three minutes," she said in a rush as she opened her briefcase on the desk. "I have to get back to court."

James opened his mouth to speak, but nothing came out. Her rushed pace and gruff tone had derailed his train of thought. "Uh—"

"Clock's ticking."

"My name's James Moore. I'm over from Kipling. You're representing a friend of mine."

Roggin looked up then, her attention finally focused on James. "Travis Wexler," she said.

"Right."

"What do you want?" She sat back in her chair and waited for him to speak. He might have her full attention for the moment, but she was clearly still in a rush.

"Well, first off, I don't think he did it."

She held up her palms. "You can stop right there. Mr. Wexler—Travis—he's admitted to this. He's legally confessed and the court has entered that confession."

"I know, but sti—"

"Mr. Wexler's been deemed legally competent, so that confession is now going to stand." She turned away and started rifling through her briefcase again.

"So what happens now?" A thread of alarm travelled through James's gut.

"Well in the next couple of weeks, the court will make its ruling official, and then he'll be remanded to the appropriate facility in compliance with that ruling." She packed files into her briefcase and then snapped it closed.

"What kind of facility? For how long?"

Roggins stood. "Let me put it this way; Travis won't be coming home any time soon. I'm sorry." She moved past him. "Now, if you'll excuse me."

He watched her hurry away, her auburn hair swishing across the back of her black suit jacket. If Travis's own lawyer couldn't—or wouldn't—help him, what was James supposed to do? He noticed the clerk looking back at him. He shrugged at her, and she gave him a quick, but sympathetic, smile.

~*~

"Don't go there, Jimmy," Duane warned

as they crossed the parking lot to the Sheriff's station.

"Why not? Isn't that what you're supposed to do? Go there? Get the facts?" Rage simmered just below the surface. Why did no one want to help Travis? Maybe he had confessed, but Duane should know better—had grown up with Travis, just like James. He should know that Travis wasn't capable of such a thing.

Duane pulled up short and spun to face James directly.

James reeled back to keep from running into Duane.

"We got the facts," Duane yelled. "He was there! He and Pearce didn't get along. Everybody knew it. He snapped, and then burned the place down to get back at the man. Then, he confessed. End of story!" He turned and headed on to the office.

James hadn't had the urge to curse in years, but a few choice expletives ran through his mind. He tamped them back knowing that profanity would neither diffuse the situation nor get him closer to answers. Why was everyone just accepting what Travis said? Had anyone interrogated him, tried to piece it all together? Or did they just accept it and let the case close, less work, more time to deal with other crimes?

He followed Duane inside and out of the cold. "So that's it? Case closed? You don't look for other, I don't know what you call it, 'scenarios'?"

Duane let out a heavy sigh. "Jimmy don't do this. Do not come back here and do this. You've been gone half a lifetime and a lot's changed. *Everything* has changed. Yes. Case closed. There are no other scenarios."

Momentary silence hung thick, and then the phone pierced the bad air between them.

Duane grabbed the receiver. "Yes?" he barked.

Trying not to eavesdrop on Duane's conversation, and irritated by the interruption, James's attention wandered the room. In the corner, a bank of filing cabinets beckoned to him. They contained all the answers Duane wasn't willing to divulge.

Duane hung up the phone. "I'm asking you, Jimmy. Stop." He moved around the table. "I'm begging you," he said in James's face. "You gotta let this go." He continued past James and out the door.

The blast of cold air grabbed hold of James's bones, and a feeling of helplessness held the chill there. He held his breath until the door had fully closed behind Duane, and then, with only a slight twinge of guilt, he slowly crossed to the filing cabinet. As he pulled open the drawer marked I-R, the thought crossed his mind that the end doesn't justify the means. "That's true, God," he mumbled aloud. "It doesn't, but what choice do I have? No one will cooperate."

He flipped through the files and found one labeled, "Pearce Fire." Another twinge of guilt pricked him as he pulled it from the drawer. He sneaked a glance towards the office door, and then tentatively opened the folder. A minute later, he replaced the folder and headed out the door. Nothing of interest or import had jumped out at him. Just a basic rundown of facts he already knew: The fire started, was reported, firefighters arrived, Travis confessed. Case closed.

He'd gone where he shouldn't go, for nothing.

Thanks a lot, God.

He didn't need a response from the Almighty to realize his frustration was misplaced, but he sure would like to catch a break sometime soon. Because he needed one to finish *this*.

10

James pulled off the road and killed the engine. As he trudged across the snow to the farmhouse, he mulled over the scant information he'd scanned in the Pearce Fire file. Basic facts: A neighbor called it in. The house was engulfed in flames when the fire department arrived. The fire had been deemed arson. Travis was on the scene—on his bicycle. Travis was questioned and subsequently confessed to starting the fire with a cigarette.

As Duane had said: Case closed.

James wandered the charred ruins of the farmhouse trying to pick up any clue at all—if not by physical evidence, then by attrition. If he winnowed what he knew until he could spot the discrepancies, then all that would be left was the truth.

And Travis would be free.

A thought crossed his mind. Travis had been at the football game prior to the fire starting. An away game...

A new gleam of hope flickered in James's

heart.

He headed for the truck.

Fifteen minutes later, he walked into the Kipling fire station. A mix of old, beat-up fire trucks sat parked next to their newer, shinier counterparts. James looked around, and found the volunteer fire chief working on the engine of one of the trucks. "Hey, Ed," James said. "You got a few minutes? I'd like to talk to you about the Pearce fire."

"Yep. Long as you don't mind me working while we talk. I gotta get this one back up and running," Ed said without taking his eye off the engine.

James nodded even though Ed wasn't looking. "Yeah, no, that's fine. I really just need to know how long it was before the Pearce house was fully engulfed."

"I don't understand the question," Ed said.

"How long would you say it was before the Pearce farmhouse was fully engulfed. You know, out of control. How long would that take?"

"That's a tough one." He paused, and the syncopated *tink* of a ratchet notching up echoed through the garage. "But we had a pretty hot end to summer and on into the fall, so everything would have been real dry. Again, it's hard to say, but I've seen places like that go up in a matter of minutes. Curtains, furniture, floorboards; no shortage of fuel."

"So what, then ten, fifteen minutes, maybe?"

Ed shrugged. "Maybe. Of course, if the fire has its way, which it often does, could be two—three—minutes, and there's nothing you can do."

"Could that have happened there?"

Ed turned from his engine work. He wiped his hands on a utility towel and eyed James with purpose. "It did, according to Travis."

James nodded in compliance, although he was still convinced things were not as they seemed. "Right. One more thing, if you don't mind."

"Startin' to, but you can ask anyway."

James held up a hand in supplication. Why was everyone so touchy when it came to this subject? " I appreciate you guys are all volunteers down here and don't imagine you have the resources you probably need, but do you keep any kind of record of what time you arrived at the Pearce fire? As exact as possible."

"You're right; we're not a cross the T's and dot the I's outfit, and I'm not sure where you're going with all this, but I do actually try and maintain some integrity around here." He crossed the garage to a metal shelving unit and then flipped open a metal index card box that was on the third shelf. "My computer," he teased as he held up the box. "Let's see here."

He pulled out a card and held it between two fingers while he dug in the pocket of his coveralls for a moment before pulling out a pair of reading glasses. "We arrived on the scene at 10:43 P.M. exactly. Our findings, as well as Travis's first-hand account tell us the fire had been going for approximately seventeen minutes at that point. That time was corroborated, give or take a minute, by Earl Jackson, who has the next farm over. He was out having a smoke. Wife doesn't let him do it in the house 'cause they got a new baby. He saw it from the get-go. He was the one who called us." Ed took off his glasses and tucked them back into his breast pocket. "There was nothing we could do. It was all but gone when we got there."

"So then, the fire started—"

"*Was* started. It didn't just magically appear, like abracadabra."

"At 10:26 or somewhere around there."

"No, *exactly* 10:26. That's when we got the call from Jackson, just as it started." Ed gave James a stony expression that clearly stated he'd taken offense at James's continued prodding.

James had meant no offense. Ed was a competent fireman and administrator; James was just trying to get at the truth. He started to say as much, but had a second think and shut his mouth.

Ed thrust his hands into the pockets of his orange coveralls. "Anything else?" The words were accommodating, but his dismissive tone didn't leave even a microdot of room for further questions.

James shook his head and turned to leave. When he stepped out into the cool air, he noted a drop in temperature. Ironically, it matched Ed's frosty reception. James's breath preceded him to the truck with each exhale.

Rationally, he understood why everyone shared Duane's "case closed" mentality; Travis had confessed, after all, but somehow the pat way in which everyone just took Travis at his word, irked James. Travis's gentle spirit was so contrary to such a deliberately heinous act, surely those who knew him should question it. *Right, God?*

Silence again.

"OK, Jimmy. Where to next?" he said aloud as he cranked the engine.

Earl Jackson.

James sped past the Pearce farm and minutes later, arrived at the Jackson acreage. A pristine late-model pickup sat in the snow-covered drive. Didn't look as if the Jacksons had left the house since the last snowfall. There were no tire tracks trailing the truck and only a thin sheet of snow had settled beneath the chassis. He pulled onto the property and parked his old truck between the newer one and a plastic snowman that sat next to the side door of the house.

Earl Jackson was shoveling snow a short distance to the west in front of a freestanding garage that did not match the pre-fab house. "Can I help you?" he called as James hopped out of the truck.

"Oh, hey," James called out as he approached Earl.

Behind him, the door to the house opened.

"You call for me?" a woman hollered.

James turned.

Mrs. Jackson was holding the door open with one hand and a swaddled baby in the other arm.

"No, sweetie, I got it," her husband answered. "It's cold out here. Go back inside." He rested a hand on the handle of the snow shovel. Once his wife was safely behind the closed door, he started towards James. "What can I do for you?"

"Hey, my name is James Moore—"

"I know who you are. Figured you'd be bigger, considering your rep'."

James suppressed a sigh. Popularity was a highly coveted commodity when he was a teen; now it was annoying, especially since he knew general consensus considered him as having abandoned the town. He'd've thought they would have forgotten him by now, put the rotting corpse of his glory days in the grave, but here was a man he'd never met—a man at least twenty years his junior—who recognized his name if not his face.

They reached each other and Earl rested his right hand on the shovel handle. "Earl Jackson."

"I'm sorry. This'll just take a minute of your time. I'm a friend of Travis Wexler."

"If it'll help you cut to the chase and get me back to work and outta this cold any sooner, Ed Beaujot called and said you might be dropping by. What do you need to know?"

Wow! He'd forgotten how fast news travelled in a town this size. Since Earl had put it so bluntly, James decided to cut right to the chase. "That night of the fire, did you see anything?"

"More than I wanted to."

"What about Travis? Did you see him, or anybody else?"

Earl looked at him as if he was Chief Moron. He pointed south into the distance. "You see those trees way over there. Plus it was night. Real dark out here at night. No. Just the fire. That's all I saw."

"So, you saw the fire and called it in." James was more thinking aloud than asking a true question. The tree line was miles away from where they were standing now.

"Right. I was out here having a smoke."

"Did you go to the Pearce place after you called?"

"Couldn't," Earl said, squinting against the sun.

"Why not?"

"Baby was inside."

James tried to hide his skepticism. "What about your wife?" he said evenly.

"What about her?"

James wondered why a simple question would put such defensiveness in the other man's tone, but he schooled his expression and his tone. "Where was she?"

Earl looked him directly in the face. "Visiting relatives."

James didn't miss the challenge in Earl's

dark brown eyes. He glanced away, far out at the tree line. "So you were out here having a smoke and your baby was inside...alone. You left the baby inside alone?"

"He was sleeping. He was fine." Earl pointed to the snow between them. "And you see that line in the ground?"

James looked down.

"Friend, you just crossed it." He shifted and lifted the shovel into his right hand. "Drive carefully," he said as he turned away. "Can't see it, but the road's all ice." He went back to shoveling snow.

Dismissed with prejudice. James hadn't quite seen that coming.

What if Earl had been the guy? Wouldn't be the first time the perpetrator was also the person who reported the crime, and Earl seemed awfully defensive for a man who just happened to see a fire start and then did the neighborly thing to save lives. Earl certainly had the means and opportunity. If his wife was gone, and since his infant obviously couldn't be a witness, Earl could have marched across the field and torched the Pearce place.

But what would have been Earl's motive?

As a counselor, James was trained to observe behavior and recognize the underlying meaning behind people's words, and he'd definitely noticed some defensive posturing from Earl. As a pastor, James was trained to hope for the best in people and to give each the benefit of the doubt, and he definitely did *not* get the hint of any motive from Earl. So why was Earl not forthcoming in helping James investigate?

Why didn't anyone want to investigate? Even the sparse police report indicated this was an open-and-shut case. But that didn't sit well. Seemed Travis had been trussed up and bow-tied like a prize pig at auction. James was beginning to think that Travis was being railroaded. Nobody wanted to investigate; they just wanted to lock Travis away and be done with it.

Case closed. Duane's words echoed again.

"Not today," James mumbled as he climbed into the cab of his truck. Today, he was going to get some answers.

~*~

The blue truck sped down the highway. James spent the time thinking over the information he'd gathered thus far. If he were honest with himself, the unraveling facts seemed to indicate a truth he didn't want to face. Duane was a level-headed man. Not prone to fancy or bigotry. So, while he might not be quick to help Travis, Duane wouldn't put the guy behind bars with no evidentiary support. *Like a flat-out confession?* Of everything he'd gathered, that confession was the most troubling. Hard to get around, but so unbelievable, just the same.

Then there was Ed. Maybe his records weren't quite right, but then why would they not be? A volunteer who took the time to keep files wouldn't then keep shoddy ones, would he? Ed could be mistaken, James supposed, but Ed was convincingly adamant about his own meticulousness.

Earl Jackson was the kicker. He reported the fire…and he was defensive about why he hadn't been on scene. What if Earl had started the fire, and then gone back to his house before calling it in?

But what motive did Earl have? Perhaps he didn't get along with Mr. Pearce. Mary said the Pearces had fit in and been beloved by the entire town; that's why the tragedy had hit everyone so hard; but then Travis and Pearce evidently didn't get along. Travis had said Pearce wanted to be rid of him. Duane had said it was common knowledge that Travis and Pearce didn't get along. It wasn't a stretch to think that Pearce may have had issues with other people.

But why would Travis confess if he didn't do it?

James sighed. He was going back and forth more often than a clock pendulum, and he felt like time was running out. Somewhere in this mess was a logical conclusion to a puzzling crime.

He drove past the green-and-white highway sign marked TAFT, and his heart rate picked up a beat. Maybe the football coach could shed some light. He made his way through town and pulled into the parking lot of Taft High School, past a parked yellow school bus and around to the large gymnasium.

A blast of cold air hit him as he hopped out of the truck and headed inside. The wind had picked up a bit in the time it had taken him to drive from Earl's. James cinched up the zipper on his coat and ducked his head.

Inside the gym, a girls' volleyball team practiced on the hard court.

James moved along the sideline and around the corner to the coach's office. The man sat at his desk writing notes. James knocked on the open door. "Coach?"

He looked up. "Yeah."

"My name's Jim Moore." He waited a beat for the coach to go all mushy with recognition, but it didn't happen. Both surprised and pleased, James gave the guy a quick smile.

"What can I do for you?"

"Looks like you got quite a team there," James said as he motioned behind him towards the gym. The squeak of sneakers on polished wood mingled with animated female voices.

"Would be if they didn't play like a bunch of girls."

James smiled. "You don't look like a volleyball guy."

"Yeah? Darn near failed science when I went here, and now I teach chemistry. We wear many hats. Welcome to public education."

"I hear you also coach varsity football."

The coach sat up straight. "Please tell me you got a kid who wants to play. I'm down to less than twenty boys most of them doing serious double duty." The expectation and hope in his tone almost made James sad to let the guy down.

"Sorry, can't help you with that."

The coach's brow furrowed. "OK, so what do you want?"

"The night you played Kipling last fall, there was a fire."

"Yeah?" he replied slowly. The coach's gaze narrowed.

James realized he was going to have to

win the guy over quickly. He took a step further inside the office. "This is gonna sound weird, but would you have any record of what time that game ended? Something official."

"What? I don't know. Why?"

"I'm just doing some follow up."

"I thought they got that crazy fella on that. It was a done deal."

Yeah, that's what everyone thought— even Travis. "Yes, well…"

"I don't understand what you're after then. You a cop, a reporter?"

"No, but I'm a minister, if that helps."

The coach took a moment to literally look James up and down, and James wondered what there was to assess. Did his calling shine from him like a halo? He very much doubted that.

"No, nobody keeps that kind of information, but I will tell you this much: Game started a little late on account of we couldn't get one of the bank of lights to go on. So instead of a seven o'clock kick off, we got going somewhere just before eight. Town ordinance says games are meant to be over and crowd dispersed by ten o'clock; I know we were a little past that."

"How far past it?"

"Not much. Maybe fifteen minutes give or take a few."

"So, the game was over by 10:15, that night? You're sure of that?"

"As sure as the fact we kicked Kipling's butt that night and that if we took any longer to do it, they'da kicked us out anyway. The one thing this town likes more than their football and hockey is their sleep."

James and the coach shared a laugh at that well-known truth, and then James headed out. Something wasn't right. The game was over at ten-fifteen, but according to Ed Beaujot, the fire had started at ten-twenty-six. That was only an eleven-minute window. Could Travis, on a bicycle, have made it from Taft to the Pearce farm in eleven minutes?

James didn't think so. And he planned to prove it.

11

"What if I can prove all this?" James picked up his pace to keep up with Paula Roggin as she raced down the hall.

The public defender stopped abruptly and turned to face him. "Mr. Moore, number one: You're not supposed to be back here. Number two: This is no longer in my hands."

"This is crazy! You're supposed to be defending him." James couldn't believe it. When he'd figured out the time window, he was sure the P.D would take the reins and help Travis.

"*Was* defending him, now I'm defending ten other people who deserve more than one overworked civil servant at Christmas who doesn't have the time or manpower to give them what they deserve either. Forget the demands of my own family."

"So that's it?" James hated the defeat that sounded in his words. He should have more resolve. More faith in the system. But then again, he'd lost his faith. So really, where did that leave him?

"Yes. That is it."

"This is insane!"

"Yes it is. Happy holidays." She turned away and left him in her wake as she disappeared down the hall in short order.

So, that was that. *Case closed.*

James let out a frustrated growl and stormed out of the courthouse. He needed to calm down, clear his head. He needed strong coffee and even stronger advice. This never-ending game of one-step-forward-two-steps-back was stretching his nerves to a thready breaking point. If the throbbing blood vessel in his temple was any indication, he would explode all over the snow-covered courthouse lawn before he ever made it back to his truck.

He thrust the keys into the ignition and then willed a deep breath and calm exterior before he fired up the engine. It wouldn't do to skid down the slicked highway and kill himself or someone else.

Pastor Barrow. The man's kind face came to James's mind. Yes; the good pastor would have great advice, and the pastor's wife brewed a mean pot of coffee.

~*~

"One half of me says let it go. Come to terms with it. The other half has no choice but to pursue it with a vengeance," James lamented forty-five minutes and three cups of coffee later. He paced the short width of the fireplace in Pastor Barrow's living room.

Mrs. Barrow sat on the couch opposite her husband, and a look passed between husband and wife that didn't bode well for James.

Pastor Barrow gave James a half-smile, one brow quirked in a trademark expression with which James was all too familiar. "I don't think 'vengeance' is the proper tack in either case. See, God has given us a free will. You know that." He leaned forward a bit. "Why is this so important to you?"

"Isn't that obvious?" The shred of aggravation which laced James's tone surprised him. Until the pastor asked the question, James had thought his motives were pure. Now he wasn't so sure. He glanced over at the pastor's wife. Didn't look as though she was too sure, either.

"Is it something more than your obvious friendship and loyalty to Travis?" the pastor pressed.

"I supposed I want to find the truth." *Pathetic!* Even as he spoke the words, James knew they weren't entirely accurate. Yes, he wanted to find the truth—for Travis's sake—but so far, the truth had made him squirm, and that was a feeling he didn't care for very much...well, not at all, actually.

"And what if the truth is exactly as they say it is?" This from the kind old woman who had nurtured James as a surrogate mother during his many visits to the pastor's house.

Her husband smiled.

James squirmed inside, the niggling like a harbinger he wanted to escape. What if Travis was guilty? How would James handle it? "Then I'll come to terms with it," he said firmly. He wasn't sure if he were trying to convince them or himself.

"Ah, but there's the rub. Can you?" Pastor Barrow asked.

As James pondered the pastor's question in stunned silence another question came to mind: Why did he want so badly for Travis to be innocent? A barrage of images flew through his mind—Travis at seven years old sticking up for another boy who was being ridiculed; Travis at ten years old running out into the street, and almost getting hit by a school bus, to shoo a dog out of harm's way; Travis at fifteen patting Karla Simpson on the back as she cried after losing the 100-metre sprint; Travis at seventeen as he grinned at James and said everything was going to be all right. James was leaving. He hadn't thought ever to return, but Travis was hopeful and happy and supportive anyway. Even though James was Travis's best friend...only friend.

And that was why proving Travis's innocence was so imperative. Because if Travis wasn't innocent, then James feared there was no innocence to be found anywhere in the world. Travis was James's last hope to believe in the greater good.

Rationally, James knew that God's goodness—the ultimate greater good—did not rest with Travis's deeds, but rationality didn't reside in James's heart right now. The only thing living there at the moment was a sense of loss and dread. His faith and his relationships were stitched together by a whisper-thin thread, his will to find meaning in the world dangled by that same thread.

That thread was Travis's innocence.

If that innocence didn't exist, James feared he'd never find meaning for his own life, he'd never mend his relationship with his father, he'd never rediscover the deep faith he'd once lived.

And then where would he be?

~*~

Snow dusted James's face as he trudged up the driveway and around to the back of the Wexler residence. After he'd left the Barrows' earlier, his mind still churning the conversations he'd had and his own motivations for investigating, he'd decided the next course of action was to see exactly how long it took to travel from Taft to the Pearce farm…on Travis's bike.

Mrs. Wexler stuck her head out the back door as he wheeled Travis's bicycle across the patio. She warmed her hands around a large coffee mug as steam rose from its contents. He gave her a nod and then hiked the ten-speed into the bed of his truck. She didn't ask anything, and he said nothing. It was as if she knew and was content with whatever James discovered.

The drive to Taft was arduous. Snow fell in a thick blanket, and James wondered if he'd be able to make the ride on Travis's bike. God smiled down, though. By the time he reached the Taft High School football field, the flurries had eased and the temperature had even warmed enough to melt the snow from the asphalt.

James parked and hauled the bike from the bed of the truck. As he straddled the seat, he checked his watch and then hit the timer.

Seconds ticked away. He peddled hard at first, but then realized Travis would not have been rushing. He'd have been travelling at a steady, comfortable pace, in no exaggerated hurry to get home.

James slowed his pace, but even still, with each rotation of the pedal, his breaths became harder to take. Closing the distance between Taft and the Pearce farm wasn't easy...and it wasn't quick.

But Travis had also said he was a little upset. The game hadn't gone well, even though Travis had stayed until the end. So maybe he'd peddled a little harder than normal. James picked up a little speed. His heart beat hard against his ribcage and his carotid pulsed hard in his neck. Breaths came in quick pants that seemed to do an ineffective job of filling his lungs with air.

How could Travis have raced this hard and then had the energy and wherewithal to set a house on fire?

James reached the Pearce farm and clicked off the stopwatch.

Thirty-two minutes, seventeen seconds. Good. That was good. That meant Travis could not have been at the farm when the fire was called in.

For good measure, though, James spent

the rest of the afternoon riding back and forth between Taft and the Pearce farm. Each time, the journey pushed exhaustion to a new level. By the time he reached the farm for the third time, he was exhausted.

Letting the bike fall sideways, he landed in the snow. His legs felt like rubber mixed with lead and tingled with pins and needles as the cold seeped through his jeans. With a hand that was shaking from cold and adrenaline, James pulled back his jacket sleeve and checked the time. His best: twenty-five minutes, three seconds.

"Oh, praise God!" He let out a sigh of relief. Still too long for Travis to have set the fire. James sank back onto the snow and rejoiced as the damp saturated his jacket and jeans. Travis was innocent; James could prove it, and he didn't have to race to Taft and back— ever again. All was right with the world.

Now, he simply had to convince Duane, the town, and Paula Roggin. And Travis.

He pedaled back to Taft at a slow pace. His body appreciated the consideration. His muscles ached from the hard push up the hill. It was odd that his last trip had been his fastest. How did his overworked legs make it up the hill faster when fatigued than when fresher the first or second runs? Maybe that was another blessing from God. The oddity only made the truth stand out more.

In the Taft parking lot, he loaded Travis's bike and then headed to Duane's office. With this new information, the good sheriff was bound to investigate further. Perhaps then, Travis would confess the truth about what happened that night.

Dusk had set in by the time James arrived at the sheriff's office. He headed inside and found Duane sitting behind his desk working on some paperwork. As James approached the desk, he pulled his notepad from his pocket and ripped the page from it that contained his travel time record.

Duane looked up at the paper outstretched in James's hand. "Hey, buddy. What's this?" He took the paper from James and scanned it.

James leaned over the desk and tapped the top of the sheet. "You see, it's all there, it's not possible! According to the Taft coach, Travis leaves the game at 10:15. Now, Travis said he didn't hang around like usual after the game, but he still stayed until the end, because he said he got out of there as soon as the horn went off to end the fourth quarter."

Duane eyed him with skepticism. He shrugged. "So? That doesn't mean he couldn't have gotten to the farm. C'mon, Jimmy. Are we going to go 'round this again?"

James clenched his jaw in a physical attempt not to rage. Was Duane serious? Even with hard evidence staring him in the face, the man wasn't going to change his view? He took in a deep breath and willed himself calm. "So then I try doing that ride, and Duane, I'm not in my best shape ever, but I rode that distance from the game to the Pearce place over and over, fast as I could. Twenty-five minutes was my best time. And I pushed that. Even if Travis beat me by five minutes, or ten even, you're looking at fifteen minutes. Add it all up, and he couldn't have gotten there by the time Ed Beaujot says that fire started. There's no way!"

James stepped back and waited for Duane to react—to come around to logical thinking. After a few moments of thick silence, James figured he needed to go on. "Look, Ed said the fire was started at 10:26. Duane, he *insisted* it started precisely at 10:26. No earlier, no later. The man wouldn't even let me say it started 'around' 10:26 he was so darn sure.

"Then, Earl Jackson said he called in the fire as soon as he saw it. He was outside having a cigarette. So Earl calls the fire in at 10:26 or right about there. Travis leaves the game at 10:15. Ride takes fifteen minutes at best. Add it up, that's 10:30! Duane, he wasn't there, at least not when Earl called it in. Couldn't've been. Even if everybody's off by a couple a minutes." James took a cleansing breath and filled his lungs with the air his rant had restricted.

Duane lifted himself out of the chair, his expression one of schooled patience that hovered somewhere between annoyance and patronization.

James remained silent and tried not to read too much in to Duane's body language.

Duane looked James in the eye. "I asked you to stop, but clearly you haven't, and I can't legally make you do anything to stop. So unless you do something stupid and make it my business, I'm just gonna step back and let you dig your own grave."

Rage traveled the length of James's body like a spark eating up real estate on a fuse. It exploded out his mouth. "Open your eyes!" He snatched the note paper from Duane's hand and headed for the door. On his way past the counter, he slapped the paper down and then gave Duane a heated look.

He stormed out the door. Nothing he could do about Duane right now, but maybe if the sheriff looked at the paper later, he'd come to his senses.

Yeah...right!

12

Silverware clinked against the ceramic plate as James cut into his meat. He glanced up at his father and shook his head. A few hours had passed since his encounter with Duane, and he still hadn't seen his heart rate return to normal. Each time he tried to let it go, something would remind him that time was running out for Travis. He couldn't even think about Travis's mother. Her acceptance of his fate was heartbreaking.

"It's good to finally hear some resolve in your voice," his father said. He took a drag off the cigarette and then slowly blew it out. "So, why do you suppose Travis would make up story like that?"

"I don't know." James chewed on a steamed carrot.

"OK, well, if not Travis, who did it?" His father's voice remained even and calm, a perfect opposite to the storm raging in James's gut.

"Maybe it was an accident. From what I

understand, it was pretty dry."

"I thought they determined it was started with a cigarette. That's what the paper said anyway. Isn't that how Travis said he started it?"

James nodded and swallowed a bite of food. "Yes sir. That part all adds up."

"Well then, the way I see it, you need to spend less time on the *why* and *how* and start focusing on the *who*."

James chewed on that while he finished the meal Mary had dropped off for him and his father. Who besides Travis could and would have set the fire? That was definitely the rub. As far as James could figure, he'd ruled out everyone else he knew. But he also knew Travis. And the man was protecting someone. It was his nature. His love of helping others was well-known. Had someone taken advantage of that and asked Travis to take the fall?

Again the idea of a conspiracy floated through James's mind. Maybe it sounded crazy, but Travis was so kindhearted that anyone with a good enough sob story might convince him to confess. The entire town thought Travis was weird, so it wouldn't take much convincing to get everyone to jump on the let's-blame-Travis bandwagon.

James helped his father clear the table and

get the dishes set in the dishwasher, and then he headed back out to the Pearce place. Maybe if he stared at the charred remains one more time, an answer would come. *Please, Lord. Your Word was right there in the ashes, God. I know You meant me to find it. Beauty from ashes, beauty from ashes...what kind of beauty could possibly come from an entire family dying in a fire?* Shards his own shattered life stabbed his being, his lost Lord, his lost friend, his lost family. James thought about his mother, what she would have done in the face of such loss. How would she feel if the tables were turned, if his father had died instead of his mother?

He considered his father as a husband losing a wife. Glen Moore had retreated behind a wall of gruffness and silence. Silence loaded with tension, feelings swirling beneath the surface as he coped with losing the love of his life. *So much loss, Lord. So much loss.* James's thoughts circled back to the Pearce family and the fire.

His truck rattled down the roadway as the wind blowing against the vehicle increased. He leaned over and dialed up the heat. Cool air pumped through the vents as the old pickup battled the cold and pushed the engine temperature. Snowflakes began to hit the windshield, but not in any number that could be deemed snowfall. For that, James was grateful. While his mind went back and forth over information, he tried to stay focused on driving, avoiding the urge to watch the snowflakes funneling in his headlight beams. He didn't want to get tunnel vision and end up in the ditch at the side of the road.

His thoughts roiled as he imagined scenarios, considered everyone he'd known when he lived here, as he tried to figure out what had happened, and why Travis was so convinced that he needed to take the blame for someone else's crime. Had Travis made another friend after James left? If so, no one had mentioned it, but then again, why would they? James made a mental note to check the visitor's log when he went to visit Travis again—see who visited. Maybe the arsonist was showing up, either to make sure Travis stayed quiet, or perhaps out of guilt or shame. James rolled his eyes and gave up his convoluted thinking. He needed to find cold, hard facts, not wild speculations on people's motives, or lack thereof.

Finally, he pulled onto the drive which led to the farm and slowly pulled to a stop near the blackened rubble. Wind whipped around his body as he plodded through the snow. The dark sky, the blowing snow, the charred rubble all contributed to the bleakness of what was left. If ever anything was needed to make someone lose all hope, this scene was it.

He tried to imagine the farmhouse before it had been burned to the ground. What had it looked like that night before the fire? What had Travis...not Travis, but rather Whoever-started-the-fire, seen that night? What had caused them to torch the place? Was someone so angry with one or all the Pearces that they thought it was worth destroying the home and everyone in it? Who would harbor such anger? James knew almost everyone in town, except the Pearces. He couldn't think of a single person who'd hold on to this much hate.

In his mind's eye, the farmhouse erected. Sturdy. Two-story. Picture windows...no, not picture windows. Old, single-paned glass set in ancient wooden frames that were painted the same white hue as the siding which covered the walls. James closed his eyes as he imagined the fire starting. Flames ignited to lick the outside walls, and then high-pitched shrieks echoed. The gruesome picture, the sounds, even the scent of the smoking ruins made his brain fill in the details. Every sense stirred, even his skin seemed to feel the heat as flames feathered up. The roar of the fire blended with the screams in his head, seemingly so real, he wanted to open his eyes and distance himself from his imaginings.

But he didn't.

Mary's words melded with the screams and the flames. They came here five years ago from England—England, no less—took over the Parker farm, and showed us a spirit like, I don't know, they just so loved being here and farming and working the land.

Loved farming. He opened his eyes and looked around at the charred furniture now illuminated in the eerie glow from his truck's headlights. *The Pearce boy, he was maybe twelve and actually wanted to grow up to be a farmer like his dad. And that's rare these days! His daughter was a few years older, really pretty. She fit right in with the other kids in town. Real pretty gal.* Mary's words reminded James that inside this home lived a normal family. His heart gave a silent scream at the loss, his eyes watered a little as empathy ripped through his soul.

Who would have wanted to hurt them?

James looked towards the field in the distance. The dark of evening did not dim the light of his imagination. He could see a bright blue day, the sun beaming onto the accommodating earth. The Pearce boy watched as his dad explained the operation of a combine, excited not only to be sharing the time with his father, but also to be learning about how to run the farm. James envisioned the son imitating the father, picking up a handful of the rich earth. He could see the father showing his son the fertile soil as he taught the child about growing food for their family, for the town, perhaps even for a hungry nation.

A normal family. Who would have wanted to hurt them?

The vision dissolved into the image of a teenage girl—the daughter. Pretty, as Mary had said. Popular as she chatted with friends on the same set of bleachers James had spotted the other teens earlier. Was she part of Ian's crowd? Or did she run in a different clique, one of so many kids in this area who loved farm life, horses and cows, learning to milk, make butter, cook, sew, the traditional home making skills taught by such organizations?

James had been to the state fair, where the kids entered all sorts of competitions and were judged on their newly acquired skills. It was a good life. *And to make it your ambition to lead a quiet life: You should mind your own business and work with your hands, just as we told you.* James mentally supplied the Scripture, 1 Thessolonians 4:11. Who had resented the Pearces doing just that?

His dad's voice faded into the scene, an

eerie voice-over in James's mind. *Well then, the way I see it, you need to spend less time on the why and how and start focusing on the who.*

"Yes, who, Lord?" James asked aloud.

An image of the Pearce children invaded his thoughts. *He was a little tough on his kids, especially the daughter—real strict with her.* Mary's words joined his father's in James's memory. Had Mr. Pearce's strictness played into things?

I thought they determined it was started with a cigarette.

His father's words dissolved the mental picture of the Pearce kids and the memory of the teens hanging out on the bleachers came back into focus. Drew—the boy who had just committed suicide; Amanda, the girlfriend. Ian...James's mind snapped back to Drew and the cigarette smoke that billowed out of that teenager's mouth.

But, the loss seemed to break him more than I think it should...Ian had nightmares every night...for months he recoiled any time someone lit a cigarette...I know they say Travis started the fire with a cigarette, but it's not as if Ian was there to see it...

Cold thrust an icy dagger into James's heart. Suddenly, the picture formed, as if James was standing right in front of the intact house. Everything coalesced into a complete story, one that clicked into place so quickly that James had to mentally back up and go over it again.

Ian *was* there to see it.

The flames in his mind's eye cooled, and James focused once again on the shattered remains of so many lives lost. But at least he believed he understood now—understood what happened, understood why Travis confessed, understood what he had to do next.

Thank You, Lord!

He hurried to his truck and headed into town. He found the teens huddled around a fire chattering to each other and totally oblivious to his presence—or perhaps just ignoring him. In the dark of night, it was difficult to believe they couldn't see his headlights shining on them.

He hunkered into his jacket. No matter, they could pretend he wasn't there, but he refused to give up. The power of his collar had given him the ability to look confident even when his heart quailed. As he approached, a burly kid turned to him.

"You want something?"

James ignored him. "Amanda, can I talk to you?" He waited, still and silent, projecting a commanding presence, a psychological stance he rarely used. But the truth needed to be told. And as sure as the sun rose in the east, James knew Amanda had the truth buried inside, the truth she desperately needed to confess.

She turned haunted eyes on him. Eyes that had witnessed something horrific, something almost worse than losing her boyfriend to suicide.

He opened his mouth to speak, but she turned away.

She couldn't even face him. Either that, or she was gathering the strength and courage to do what she had to do. Somehow, she seemed to know what he was about to ask.

"Amanda, I know what happened that terrible night, and you have nothing to be afraid of if I'm right. You were there that night, weren't you? You, Drew,"—he scanned them all—"Maybe all of you were there. But you were there, weren't you?"

She just stared at him, fear glazing over her eyes as she hugged herself.

He wanted to believe she was just protecting her body from the icy temperature, but James knew better.

Like a small creature trembling before a predator she shivered, her devastated soul haunting her whole being.

"You were trying to get the Pearce girl to hang out. I mean, it's Friday night—the weekend, right? But she couldn't, could she? 'Cause her old man kept her on a tight leash."

He took a step forward to close the distance between them. "So there you are, trying to get her to sneak out maybe. Drew probably, acting crazy, leading the charge. And he was smoking wasn't he? Even I saw him with a cigarette in his mouth. And then her old man shows up, doesn't he? And he's angry. Probably real angry. Tells you to get outta there. But Drew gets in his face..."

James broke off and took another few steps towards the huddle.

They didn't move, but he sensed them tightening up, held together by a tragedy they'd all witnessed and couldn't quite handle. They closed ranks, without moving a muscle. Nobody was talking.

He needed answers, and they needed absolution. But he didn't want to scare them all, either. They were just kids. Whatever happened, he had to remember they were kids and sometimes, kids made horrible mistakes. He took a breath and watched the fog billow out his mouth. "But he won't let it go, will he? He just keeps pushing, showing off for you guys." He waited a beat, hoping Amanda or one of the others would confirm his suspicions. No one said a word, but a sheen of tears glistened in Amanda's eyes.

"Now this is the part I'm not sure about,"

James said, "but it was Drew's cigarette that started that fire, not Travis's, right?" He lowered his voice. "So, did he mean to do it?"

"It was an accident." Ian appeared from out of the shadows, his face in a scowl, his voice barely audible.

James looked into his nephew's eyes and noted the relief, the need to pass the burden to someone else, to confess, to purge his soul's desperate need for expiation, for redemption. *Thank You, God, for giving me a break in this case…please take care of Ian's soul, too…all of these kids…please let them know that You love them and nothing will make that go away…*With that prayer, James felt the stumbling block within his own heart lighten, as if the children's needs had opened a door in his soul.

"Shut up, man" the burly kid said.

"What?" James said to Ian.

"It was an accident! It was just an accident. It was an accident," Ian hollered. He shuffled forward, his entire body a limp and dejected.

Tears spilled onto Amanda's cheeks, and James reached for her. Seconds passed before she decided to accept his embrace, but the she launched into his arms, sobbing uncontrollably. Her whole body trembled. James didn't say anything as he held her. But he knew she had to release all the sadness, the terror, the whole aloneness that had suffocated her from the day of the fire, through her boyfriend's death, to now. He had plenty of experience with grief, his own and those he counseled. It never got any easier to bear or to hear.

"He didn't mean to do it. We tried to help but... I'm so scared. I'm so sorry. What's gonna happen? What's gonna happen? I'm so scared. Help, please help."

Her body shivered in his arms, and James's heart broke for her, for them all. "It's OK. You're OK. It's all over."

He pulled back to look at her, and she smacked away her own tears.

"You know we have to tell the sheriff the truth, right? We can't let Travis take the blame for this."

She nodded as she hiccoughed on a sob.

He raised his gaze to the others. Relief shone in every eye. These kids had borne a burden that had crushed lesser people. A horrible accident had transformed them into children who thought they had no future beyond the horror that hung over them. Giving the burden to him...to a minister, whom they thought had a direct line to God, had set them free.

...and you will know the truth, and the truth

will set you free. The verse from John's Gospel travelled through James's head, and he said a silent prayer of thanks. Despite the cold night, warmth blanketed James. God had not abandoned him after all, He'd led him home and to the facts that would free Travis—and ease the burdens these teens had carried for so long.

James's heart suffused with God, the Almighty lighting the places that had darkened, filling him with such joy that tears gathered at the corners of his eyes, although none fell. He took a deep breath and let it out.

With light shed on the truth, the entire town could heal. The Pearces were still gone; nothing could ever change that, but surely, an accident would be easier to bear than one of their own committing murder. Justice would repair the damage, forgiveness would heal them all.

Is this why you led me home, Lord?

The silent prayer again went unanswered, but this time James was not discouraged. Something inside him was restored, replenished. God's silence wasn't empty, it was comfortable—they were like old friends again, content to be in each other's company without having to utter a word.

And in the middle of the winter snow,

surrounded by young men and women he hardly knew, and with his Heavenly Father mute as a mouse, James felt the comfort of home.

13

"It's OK." James coaxed Amanda to speak.

She stood near the window looking past the glass and into the pristine, morning snow. She glanced at him, then Mrs. Wexler, and then Duane and Ian.

James wondered if she were nervous because of what she was about to confess or because her mother had told her to come alone. Whatever the cause, Amanda was facing her future.

James glanced at Ian, and then set his gaze briefly on his sister. She looked worried, and for that, James was sorry. He couldn't ease the pain he knew Mary was going through at discovering her son had been lying to her all these months, but he admired her courage and loyalty. He expected nothing less. Mary had learned from their mom to nurture and love, and she did both with equal power. No matter what happened, she was here for Ian.

Did that make it harder for Amanda?

James cross the room and touched the young girl's arm. "Please, Amanda."

She gave him a half-smile, and then looked at Duane. "It was an accident." She shrugged. "We went to see if Beth-Ann could hang with us, but nobody answered the door. So we go around back to her bedroom window, you know; and Drew's tossing rocks at it and hollering…you know how he could be sometimes. You hauled him in here enough," she said to Duane. "But Beth, she just waves us off, and then Mr. Pearce comes to the window and tells us to take off." She paused for a moment and shared a look with Ian.

He nodded almost imperceptively.

She turned back to Duane. "Drew went nuts. He starts all hollering and posing, yelling at Beth to come out. Yelling at Mr. Pearce that he couldn't do anything to stop us." Her brow furrowed.

"We all wanted to leave, but Drew wouldn't let it go." Ian picked up the story.

Amanda didn't seem to mind. She turned her attention to the landscape outside the window. Her body language suggested she was at peace, the horrific burden of keeping the secret gone.

James figured she'd probably replay the events for some time, and have a deep regret that never went away, but with the story out in the open, people would judge or not, and she'd stand up to it, knowing she'd told the truth.

"Mr. Pearce says we got to the count of three, and Drew, he just starts mocking Mr. Pearce, putting on this fake English accent. 'One, two, three, four, five, six…what're you waiting for' he says. 'This guy needs a wake-up call,' he says to us." Ian shook his head. "We were trying to leave. Begging Drew to come on. But he just kept pounding on the house and yelling stuff. 'I ain't scared of you!' he yells at the house. Then, he flicked his cigarette." Ian looked at his mother. "I tried to get him to leave." He shared a look with Amanda. "We all did."

Ian focused on Duane once again. "I decided I was going to leave, but when I rounded the house, I saw the fire. Drew's cigarette. I was so scared! 'Drew, get over here' I yelled. He came straight away but, man, that fire spread quick."

Amanda nodded. "The flames were everywhere, and then windows started busting out.

"Drew hollered for Andy to call 911, but there was no reception." Amanda paused and broke into a short sob. "And then everyone was screaming…them inside, us outside. I was so scared. I didn't know what to do."

"Then everybody took off. It was like we all knew it was over, and we didn't want to get busted," Ian offered. "I grabbed Amanda, and we all jumped in the truck and bolted."

"But, it was an accident, Sheriff. I swear it," Amanda added.

James gave her a sympathetic look. "It's going to be OK." He turned to Duane. "I figure that's when Travis shows up, heart pounding from his ride, he sees the fire. But Travis is Travis. Afraid or not, he gets back on his bike and pedals toward that house with every ounce of strength and energy he can muster. Whatever fear he's feeling is won over by the goodness that's always been in his heart.

"But by the time he gets there, there's nothing he can do. The flames are out of control...I can only imagine what must have been going through his head. Not being able to help must've been his worst nightmare..." James let his voice trail off as the mental image formed of Travis standing helpless amongst the flames. Travis, whose goal in life was to help anyone who needed it.

Duane rested his hips against the desk. "OK, so why the lie? The confession?"

"I don't know. Maybe he felt guilty that he couldn't do anything...he couldn't save them."

The room fell silent for a moment.

"No. He sacrificed himself for us. He was saving *us*." Amanda's soft voice broke the stillness, creating a palpable awe.

This is my commandment: love one another as I love you. No one has greater love than this, to lay down one's life for one's friends. Jesus' words from John's Gospel reverberated in James's heart. And James suddenly knew the truth of it, the truth of Amanda's words, the truth that had always, always been his friend, Travis. Even without deliberation, Travis lived God's greatest commandment without hesitation. Unwavering faith...Innocent and complete devotion to what was right.

James looked at Amanda.

She smiled gently and then looked away and out the window. Sunlight sparkled through the glass sending a sheen of beauty across Amanda's face. Her tranquil, peaceful face, as if she shared an understanding moment with James. No, with God. *No one has greater love than this, to lay down one's life for one's friends.* Amanda knew not only what Travis had done, but also why. If her expression was anything to go by, Travis's sacrifice for her had brought Amanda out of her darkness and to a deeper understanding of her Creator.

The Lord truly was amazing, guiding, protecting, reassuring in ways James had forgotten—almost abandoned.

But not today. Hopefully, not ever again.

He glanced at Ian as the boy rested his head on Mary's shoulder. She comforted her son with a motherly embrace that Ian did not balk at—despite his age and gender. In the age old gesture, Ian cemented the need for his mother, the love that God had infused into Mary's heart, for such a time as this. The overwhelming love he had for his sister's strength made tears threaten, but James held it in. Barely.

From the corner, Mrs. Wexler's face beamed with joy. "Thank you," she said softly.

"OK," Duane said, breaking the emotional moment. "Let's see if we can get the DA and Public Defender's office on the phone, so we can get Travis outta that place."

~*~

James helped Travis load his suitcase into the bed of the truck, and then they got inside. One last look at the formidable building brought a shiver to James's body, as he contemplated what the rest of Travis's life could've looked like. No matter how calm Travis was, no matter his acceptance of that fate, James was glad his friend would not have to endure it ever again.

They travelled in silence most of the way home. What had started as a sunny day turned to a decent, steady snowfall by the time they reached Kipling city limits, and James paid close attention to the road while the passing scenery outside the truck held Travis's attention.

At the house, James exited the truck and grabbed Travis's bag out of the back. The leather was soaked and dark in spots, but probably not all the way through.

Travis came around the back of the truck. "I suppose I don't need to say it, but thank you, Jimmy." He took his bag.

"Aw, c'mon Travis. Doesn't make up for half the stuff you've done for me."

Travis grinned. "Well then, all's even in the world once again. You scratch my back, and I'll scratch yours."

James patted Travis on the back and gave a little scratch. "Sounds like a plan."

"Sounds like a plan," Travis repeated. He trudged through the snow to the front door.

"Hey, you know you could've just told Duane that it was an accident in the first place."

Travis turned and twisted his face into a sheepish grin. "Yeah, I started thinkin' about that sittin' in that tiny little cell thinkin' *this tiny little cell stinks*."

James chuckled.

The front door opened, and Mrs. Wexler looked out.

Travis turned to look at her, and her face split into a wide, delighted grin.

James imagined Travis smiling back, but when he turned, his expression was sober. "Naw. Even if everyone believed me, those kids would've been looked at funny their whole lives because everyone would've still wondered what really happened. It's no piece a cake going through life, people looking at you funny like that, trying to figure out your secrets. They didn't need that..." He shrugged. "'Sides, I figured everyone's been wanting to get rid of me so bad, and no one knew how to do it...I'd just do it for them."

"Nobody wants to get rid of you, Travis," James said.

A hint of Travis's smile returned. "Yeah, right."

"Well, one thing at a time." James shrugged and then lifted the collar of his jacket.

"Sounds like a plan," Travis said. He turned and disappeared behind the front door.

Epilogue

Christmas day

James touched the clerical collar at his throat. It felt good to be back. *Thank You, again, Lord.* There really were no words to describe the fullness of his soul, the sense of belonging, being one with his Lord again, but God knew, and for that, James was grateful. He, a man who preached the Word, was at a loss for words before his God, but everything was written on his heart, and God would read it, as He always did.

The church, decorated for the season with festive garland and sprigs of holly, set the mood for worship. The light suffused through the building, bringing hope on wings of reverence. There was excitement in the air, a renewed sense of purpose. The pall that had hung over this town for so long was gone. *The truth shall set you free...*

James smiled at Pastor Barrow and his wife, sitting to the side of the altar; then he smiled out at the congregation. So many familiar, friendly faces: Amanda, Duane, Dad, and Mary and the kids…and Travis.

James looked down at the pulpit. "The spirit of the place astounds the joy of it all. The reception bestowed upon us is surely of Your making and the generosity of those who have received us. We are blessed to be here, to use our hearts and hands to honor, to serve, to sow the seed.

"All men walk in the shadows of uncertainty, and it was with anxious concern that we set forth on our journey. We have been taught that it is without faith that we stumble and fall and cannot get up; and it is without community that we fear the darkness. But here, in this remote freckle on your bountiful earth, we have found solace. We have found a comfort among strangers and a beacon of light from a community so strong that no shadow shall do us harm, no matter how wide it's cast. Nor shall it prevent us from living the life You have created for us to serve in Your name and to enjoy Your wondrous and abundant gifts. We thank You Lord, in the Name of Jesus Christ, for the opportunity before us. Your humble and faithful servant"—he looked up at the congregation—"Samuel Pearce."

In the silence held by the congregation,

James held up the charred Bible he'd found at the Pearce farm.

Gasps rolled across the congregants as realization took hold.

James stepped from the pulpit and moved to the center of the altar. "From the ashes of that tragedy: Lasting words. A personal preface to the everlasting words of God, Almighty. You see, the dark events that happen in our lives, those aren't hurdles He puts before us to see how high we can jump or how hard we stumble. No, our God is more loving than that, He's smarter than that.

"No, those hurdles are the way we *choose* to look at the bad stuff in our lives, those dark shadows that cast doubt and fear. All too often we get so caught up, so intertwined and knotted up in the threads of our lives we forget to look at the bigger picture, the entire weaving of His fabric.

"Now I don't know about you, but when I pull those covers over me on a cold winter's night, I don't want to depend on one single, measly, tiny little thread to keep me warm. No, I want that entire blanket to smother me and comfort me. If I don't, I'll freeze my butt off!"

Chuckles filled the church.

"And that's the way God works. Not thread by thread, but the entire weaving, His warmth, His Being. And for that, He wants one thing and one thing only—our faith. Our unbroken belief and infinite trust in the journey that He has planned for us. No matter how challenged we may feel, whatever dark shadow we may find ourselves cast under no matter, how rusted the squeaky hinge, He is there for us, fighting that rust that works its way into all our lives, smothering us with his unconditional and everlasting blanket of warmth and comfort."

He smiled out, and then gave a nod to Pastor Barrow. With one final look back at the crucifix hanging on the wall behind him, James stepped off the altar to take his place among the congregation while Pastor Barrow concluded the Christmas service.

Thanks be to God, he was home. Kipling had had its share of triumph, of love, of pain and loss, but they'd weathered it all because the goodness of one simple man, who was willing to shoulder a burden that wasn't his, who'd lain down his life in honor of his God. The same God who'd help James see that sometimes, where there is great loss, beauty could come from ashes. He was home, and the rusty hinges of his faith were oiled and shined to reveal the future ahead—a future filled with purpose, with family and with friends.

About the Author

Corbin Bernsen comes from an entertainment family. His mother, who recently passed away, had been on the long running soap *The Young and Restless* for 35 years. A graduate of UCLA where he earned a Bachelor's degree in Theater and a Master's degree in Playwriting, he most recently starred as Henry Spencer on USA Network's hit original series *PSYCH*. He was first catapulted to stardom during the 1980s by the hit NBC TV series, *L.A. Law*. Twice, he was nominated for both an Emmy® Award and a Golden Globe Award® for his performance as Arnie Becker on the show that virtually created the ensemble drama as we know today. Along the way he hosted *Saturday Night Live,* and guest starred on *Seinfeld* and *Star Trek* to name a few notable television appearances. In the feature film arena, he starred in the comedy *Hello Again*, followed by other critically acclaimed roles in *Disorganized Crime*, Wolfgang Peterson's *Shattered*, The Great White Hype, and as the Cleveland Indians' third baseman-turned-owner Roger Dorn in the extremely popular *Major League* series of films. Other film credits include *Lay the Favorite* with Bruce Willis and *The Big Year* with Steve Martin, Jack Black and

Owen Wilson. He also appeared with Robert Downey Jr. and Val Kilmer in *Kiss Kiss Bang Bang*. Recently, Bernsen has moved to the other side of the camera, directing the films *Carpool Guy*, *Dead Air* and *Rust*, which was distributed by Sony Pictures Entertainment. With *Rust*, Bernsen shifted his focus to family friendly movies and formed Home Theater Films. *25 Hill*, which he also wrote and directed, is the first title from his newly formed company and was distributed by EchoLight Studios in July 2012. This was followed by *3 Day Test* (2012) and *Beyond the Heavens* (2013), also released by EchoLight Studios. Bernsen latest project, *Christian Mingle*, was just released in January 2015 by Capitol. Bernsen lives in Los Angeles with his wife of twenty-six years, actress Amanda Pays, and their four sons.

About RUST the Movie

The movie, which Francine Brokaw of Family Magazine Group calls "a shining story of rediscovering faith" is still available for purchase through local and online retailers or directly from Home Theater Films (http://hometheaterfilms.com). Pick up your copy today.

Screenplay
Corbin Bernsen

Producers
Corbin Bernsen, Chris Aronoff, Dana Lesiuk

Director
Corbin Bernsen

Starring
Corbin Bernsen, Lorne Cardinal,
Lloyd Warner

Running time
95 Minutes

Rated
PG

Discussion Questions

1. James leaves his clerical shirt and collar on the pew when he leaves the church. Discuss the symbolism within his soul and what others might think. Is he leaving the ministry behind because he feels compelled to a new calling or is he simply running away? Can you relate to James's actions?

_____

_____

_____

_____

_____

_____

_____

_____

_____

_____

_____

_____

2. Discuss the correlation between James leaving his Heavenly Father behind while, at the same time, he works up the courage to face and repair the relationship with his earthly father. Is it easier to mend an earthly relationship or the spiritual relationship with the Almighty?

_____

_____

_____

_____

_____

_____

_____

_____

_____

_____

_____

_____

3. When James's father brushes him off in the barn, it brings a moment of clarity to James's own recent past. Discuss the aspects of finally recognizing when the heart begins to heal. How do you handle those oftentimes difficult epiphany moments?

_____

_____

_____

_____

_____

_____

_____

_____

_____

_____

_____

_____

4. In the truck, James finally recognizes that his family and most of the townsfolk were affected in various ways by the fire and the subsequent loss of lives. Discuss how James can identify the problem outside himself but not his own lack of faith and commitment. How has his loss of faith changed him?

_____

_____

_____

_____

_____

_____

_____

_____

_____

_____

_____

_____

5. Have you ever felt so broken, so helpless and so despairing, that it seemed as if nothing matters? Did you turn to God in those times? Did you receive no as an answer, peace as an answer...or a miracle?

_____

_____

_____

_____

_____

_____

_____

_____

_____

_____

_____

6. When James realizes his family doesn't trust him, he becomes bitter, but then he realizes that it is he who broke faith with them. Have you ever experienced an epiphany that confirms you were in the wrong? How did you handle it?

_____

_____

_____

_____

_____

_____

_____

_____

_____

_____

_____

_____

7. Have you ever been someone's knight in shining armor, sacrificed yourself or something else of value in order to save their reputation? If so, what were your secret misgivings, if any? If not, under what circumstance would you be willing to sacrifice for another?

_____

_____

_____

_____

_____

_____

_____

_____

_____

_____

_____

_____

8. Have you ever been or felt responsible for someone else's actions? How did you handle the responsibility—with charity or begrudgingly, or did you run away completely? When God tells us to watch out for each other, to be our brothers' keeper, do you think it is fair? Why or why not?

_____

_____

_____

_____

_____

_____

_____

_____

_____

_____

_____

_____

Thank you...

for purchasing this Harbourlight title. For other
inspirational stories, please visit our on-line
bookstore at www.pelicanbookgroup.com.

For questions or more information, contact us at
customer@pelicanbookgroup.com.

Harbourlight Books
The Beacon in Christian Fiction™
an imprint of Pelican Ventures Book Group
www.pelicanbookgroup.com

Connect with Us
www.facebook.com/Pelicanbookgroup
www.twitter.com/pelicanbookgrp

To receive news and specials, subscribe to our
bulletin
http://pelink.us/bulletin

May God's glory shine through
this inspirational work of fiction.

AMDG